LITTLE
ORPHAN ANNIE
and the
Gila Monster Gang

A Story Based on the
Famous Newspaper Strip
"LITTLE ORPHAN ANNIE"
By Harold Gray

Authorized Edition

WHITMAN PUBLISHING COMPANY

RACINE, WISCONSIN

ILLUSTRATIONS

TABLE OF CONTENTS

Little Orphan Annie and Sandy Walked up the Road

LITTLE ORPHAN ANNIE

and the
Gila Monster Gang

CHAPTER ONE

THE DESERTED MINE

Little Orphan Annie sat down wearily on a big stone at the side of the little mountain road, dropping down beside her the big bandanna handkerchief which held her few possessions.

"Gee, Sandy," she said to her dog, "do you suppose we took the wrong road? We haven't seen a house or a car for miles, let alone finding a town. I feel as though we'd been climbing straight up since the first thing this morning."

Sandy had plopped himself down beside her. Now he buried his head between his two paws as if he too were tired of looking at the stony road.

"Well, we've got to find some place to spend the night pretty soon. We can't stay out on top of a mountain once the sun goes down. We'd freeze in no time. Come on, we can't sit here. Maybe there will be a place over that next rise."

Reluctantly Sandy got up and Annie, feeling discouraged, started slowly up the road.

"You know, Sandy," she said to her dog, "always think there's something good just over the next hill. Some people always look for something bad just out of sight where they can't see it, and nine times out of ten they find it. I'll bet we find a nice little house just over the top of this hill, with smoke coming out of the chimney, and a path leading up to its door."

Sandy wagged his tail. Any place would suit him, just so he could sit down for a while. Annie had been a hard taskmaster who kept him moving pretty steadily all day. It really had been harder on Annie than it had on Sandy, but she was not one to complain. Every once in a while she had to stop to pick a stone from the hole in the bottom of her shoe, and though she would not admit it even to herself, it felt as if there were a blister on her heel.

Annie was a game youngster though, and this walking from place to place was not exactly new to her. She had been on the road for almost two weeks. As the last few feet of uphill going came, Annie decided to get the suspense over. She ran as fast as she could to the top of the rise.

"Sandy, what did I tell you? Here's the path! I knew we'd find something over the hill."

Sandy was not as enthusiastic as Annie. Yes, there was a path, a little overgrown one that looked as though it hadn't been used for years, but there was no sign of a house. Sandy would have preferred going on down the road. It was downhill going now, and easier, and at least there was a road, for he could see it stretch away into the distance. He ran ahead a little way, but Annie couldn't be persuaded to change her mind.

"Come on, Sandy. It's a path. It's got to go somewhere and I don't see any other house down there, do you? Come on, I'm not going to wait for you any longer. We've been on that old road long enough. I should think you'd be sick of it, too."

She swung her bundle up over her shoulder and started down the trail. Not convinced, but unable to change Annie's mind, Sandy followed her. The path wound between low scrub pine and wind-twisted oaks. Once they had to crawl cautiously over a big boulder that had fallen across the path. It looked as if it had lain there a long time, and that should have warned Annie that there wouldn't be much to see at the end of the trail, but Annie was so anxious to find some shelter for the night that she ignored the sign. They had to jump over a fast-flowing little stream, and Sandy stopped to take a long drink, but Annie couldn't wait. She wanted to find the end of the path. Finally, around an especially sharp turn in the path they caught sight of an old tumble-down building. It was a large place, but from the outside it looked as if it were just one big room. Annie looked around to see if she could find any signs of life, but everything was still.

"Gee, Sandy, maybe you were right. Maybe we should have stayed on the road. Leapin' lizards, that place doesn't look as though it had been used for years." She gave a shiver. "It sure looks spooky, doesn't it?"

Sandy was not especially anxious to go exploring. He pushed himself close to Annie's skirts and together they went cautiously toward the building.

"I don't know what's wrong with us, Sandy." Annie was trying to get back her courage, but she was talking in a whisper, as though someone might hear her in this desolate place. "There isn't a sign of anyone around. Certainly they wouldn't care if we stayed for a night. It isn't much, but at least the wind wouldn't hit us the way it does out here."

She reached the doorway, and looking first to be sure there was no one around, she pushed the door open and peeked in.

It was just what it had appeared from the outside, one great big room. There was an old wood stove at one end, with a trestle table near it. Two chairs had been pushed back into the corner near the stove, and the scattered parts of others showed that they had served someone as fuel for the fire. Overhead Annie saw streaks of light coming from gaps in the roof where boards had fallen away.

"Gosh, it's old enough, Sandy, and it's not so good, but it doesn't look as though anyone would bother us, nor we bother anyone else. I guess we'd better stay here tonight. At least we've got a roof over our heads." Looking up at the light coming through the holes she amended her statement, "At least, it's half a roof."

She got to work immediately. Tired as she was, she walked back to the little stream and filled her bucket with water. Annie knew it would soon be dark, and she would certainly lose her way if she tried to find the stream at night. On the way back to camp she picked up a few branches for her fire.

Back in the house she piled her branches in the stove and touched a match to them. "It's good I've still got matches with me. They certainly come in handy. I'm afraid I'm not much of a Girl Scout when it comes to starting a fire with sticks."

From her small store of supplies in the bandanna she took a can of beans. "Do you remember the fellow that gave us this, Sandy?" she asked, holding the can up for the dog to see. "That was the storekeeper back near the railroad station. He said he couldn't sell it anyway because it was dented, but I'll bet he was just being kind. Anyhow, I'd kiss him for it if he were here right now. It'll sure taste good when I get it heated."

Setting the can over the fire, she wandered around

the room to see if she had missed anything. Suddenly she let out a startled little shriek. Sandy, who had settled down close to the stove to rest and get warm, jumped into the air, his hair bristling. Good protector that he was, he rushed over to Annie. She stood there, her eyes popping at a big pile in the corner. To Annie it looked like a man flopped down and covered with dirty blankets. Sandy gave her his wide dog grin. He had examined that pile long ago, but not until he had gone over and pulled away one of the blankets would Annie approach. It was just a pile of dirty blankets, filled with the dust of years. Why they had been left, or why the people who had broken up the chairs for kindling hadn't taken them was a mystery, but there they were.

"Golly, I'm getting to be an awful scaredy cat, Sandy. I could have sworn there was a man under those blankets. Did you know they were there all the time?"

Sandy wagged his tail, happy to have Annie admire his courage.

"Well, I'm sure glad they're here. I wondered how cold we'd get with nothing to cover us. It gets pretty cold this high in the mountains. They're awfully dirty, but I can give them a good shaking."

She gathered the pile in her arms, and though the dust made her sneeze she shook the blankets at the doorway until the clouds of dust cleared away. Her

arms were completely worn out. Sandy, finding that
the dust made him sneeze, too, retreated to the stove,
his eyes watering, and sat down to watch the supper.
When Annie brought the pile of old blankets back
to the room she discovered him sitting there, his eyes
never leaving the can on the fire.

"Yes, I know you're hungry, Sandy, and I suppose
those beans are hot by this time."

She dusted off a place on the table, using a piece
of blanket which was not big enough to be used as
a covering. Her bandanna would serve as a table-
cloth. Then she carefully opened the beans. She had
four hard rolls in her store.

"We'll eat one apiece tonight, and that will leave
us two for breakfast," she told her dog. "Beans and
bread and nice cold water make a pretty good meal."

She carefully marked the can so that she would
not get more than her share, and started eating.
When she reached the halfway point she broke up
the other roll and set the can on the floor for the dog.
Sandy, his tail waving as fast as he ate, finished the
food in no time at all.

While Sandy was eating, Annie went to the door
to look out over the mountains.

"Gee, Sandy, just look at the sunset. I never saw
one from the top of a mountain before. It's like being
right in the center of it. I'll bet the people down in
the valleys miss this completely. It's—it's as though

we were being told there was someone who would protect us and watch over us. Do you suppose everyone who sees a sunset feels as though it belonged just to him?"

Together the two, girl and dog, sat down on the rickety step to watch the beautiful spectacle. It was not till the rose and blue tones had turned to deep purple, and the mountain wind came around the corner of the building with the added strength it gains when the sun goes down, that they went back into the building.

Putting the remaining twigs on the fire, Annie spread out the blankets in front of the old stove, pulled off her uncomfortable shoes, and dragging Sandy close to her for warmth, settled down for the night.

Before she slept she thought of all the things that had happened to her since Daddy Warbucks had left to work for Uncle Sam.

"Golly, I'm glad he thinks I'm safe and well taken care of. He'd worry himself sick if he thought I was traveling around this way. He thinks I can't take care of myself, and it's nice of him to fuss over me, but when I have to I can do a pretty good job of looking after myself. I hope he's safe. If only I could write to him and tell him not to worry I'd feel better."

Feeling blue, she turned her mind to other thoughts, and looking up through the openings in the roof she saw the first star twinkling down at her. It was as near as the sunset had seemed, and comforted by its companionship she put an arm around Sandy and fell asleep.

The first rays of the sun woke her next morning. One very persistent little beam found its way through a hole in the roof and settled itself right in Annie's eyes. She woke with a start. For a moment she couldn't remember where she was, and then the sunbeams dancing above her reminded her of the star of the night before. She sat up, stretched, and looked around, brave with the thought that there was always Someone looking after her. Sandy was up before her, and just as she began to wonder what had become of him, he poked his nose in through the door. It was a very wet nose and Annie laughed at him.

"So you had to go get yourself a drink. Well, you'll just have to walk back again with me. You're not the only one who's thirsty this morning."

She picked up her shoes and looked sadly at the gradually widening holes in the soles.

"These aren't going to last much longer, Sandy. I don't know what I'll do when they give out completely."

Suddenly she had an idea. With her knife she cut pieces from the blanket rag she had used as a duster the night before.

"This won't last as long as leather, but it will be better than nothing," she said, cutting busily with her knife until the pieces fitted smoothly into the shoes. She put them on, wiggled her toes to be sure the pieces would be comfortable, and with a proud sigh at her handiwork galloped down the path toward the creek.

She washed her face and hands and took a deep drink of the ice-cold water. Then shivering she raced back to the cabin.

She carefully folded the blankets and put them back in their corner.

"Now the next person who sees them won't think they're a man the way I did," she said, surveying the neat pile.

She looked around to be sure everything was the way they had found it. Then she opened her bandanna and looked at their last two rolls.

"Shall we eat them now, or leave them till noon?" she asked Sandy, and Sandy, always hungry, wagged his tail at the word "eat." Annie, reluctant to part with their last bit of food, finally compromised with her hunger and broke one roll carefully in half, saving the other one for noon. This she folded in her bandanna, and all ready to leave they sat on the doorstep and munched their hard roll. It was then that Annie noticed a path going from the cabin down the mountain. That, like the one to the cabin, was all overgrown, but Annie was always curious, and still chewing on the last bite of roll, she picked up her bandanna and started down the trail.

"Come on, Sandy, let's explore. Maybe we can get down the valley this way instead of going back to the road."

Sandy, who had been so hesitant the night before about going exploring, was perfectly willing to lead the way today.

They raced down the path, jumping over the rocks and branches that barred their way. They had not gone far, however, when they had to slow down. The trail had become a narrow ribbon along the side of the mountain, and to their right was a long drop down into a deep ravine. Annie began to wonder if they should not turn back and find the road they had been following the day before, but Sandy, sure-footed and paying no attention to the drop beside him, followed the path. Annie, not to be outdone by her dog, followed him, trying not to look down over the edge of the path.

Suddenly Sandy pricked up his ears and stopped. Annie, knowing that his keen ears could hear more than hers could, listened carefully. She could hear nothing at first, but then very faintly she could hear the whistle of a train down in the valley below them. She could not see it, but a train down there meant some sort of town, or at least some people.

"Maybe this is the way down, Sandy, only I should think people would rather take the road than this narrow little path. Do you suppose if you're born in the mountains this kind of path is just natural to you? I sure don't feel very comfortable on it."

She edged her way carefully around a turn, holding on to the rock beside her. Not until she was safely around the corner would she let herself look down. Then she saw across the valley from her a building similar to the one in which they had spent the night.

"We've gone round in a circle, Sandy," she exclaimed. "That's the place we slept last night."

Sandy, wagging his tail, continued down the path, and Annie, not knowing what else to do, followed him. She soon discovered that the path they were on went down the ravine, then up the other side to the house, and it certainly wasn't the path they had been on the day before. As the path went down farther into the ravine it no longer followed the side of the cliff and Annie found it much easier walking. It took no time at all to get across the ravine and up the other side to the building.

Like the one they had been in, it had stood empty for years. Annie hesitated as she neared it, as she had the night before, but, telling herself that this building was probably as deserted as the other one had been, she peeked through a knothole in the wall. It was dark, but not entirely so, for the roof let in some

Annie Edged Her Way Around a Turn

daylight. This cabin was unlike the other one, though. Huge timbers supported the ceiling, and in the center of the room was a big hole through the flooring.

"Leapin' lizards, Sandy, am I dumb. You know what this is? It's a mine. There's the shaft that goes down. I should have known that in mountains like this we'd find some mines. Come on, let's see what it looks like inside. It seems as deserted as the cabin."

She pushed the door open carefully. Inside it seemed darker than it had from the outside, but soon her eyes became accustomed to the darkness, and going cautiously over to the shaft she knelt down and looked over the edge. Sandy, too, put his nose over the edge to peer down, but just as he did, something black whooshed past his nose.

"Whew," said Annie, jumping back from the hole.

Sandy, his tail between his legs, rushed for the door. Then Annie, realizing what had passed them, began to laugh.

"Now who's the coward, Sandy? Those were nothing but old bats. Come back here! Maybe a mountain trail scares me, but I'm not going to be afraid of a couple of *harmless bats*."

Sandy, not able to remind her of her fear of a pile of blankets, came back wagging his tail and bravely stuck his nose over the edge again. Nothing at all happened this time and they had a good chance to look down the shaft.

"When the mine was working I suppose they had a windlass and machinery here to pull the elevator up," Annie explained to Sandy.

Now there was nothing but a rickety old ladder leading far down into the black hole.

"Do you suppose that ladder would hold me?" asked Annie. She sat down at the top and put all her weight on the first rung. It held. She turned around so that she was facing the ladder, and holding tightly to the sides started down.

Sandy whimpered at the top. "Oh, don't make such a fuss," ordered his mistress. "I'm all right."

But Sandy wouldn't be comforted. He ran back and forth at the top of the ladder and then put his two front feet on the first round.

"Hey," yelled Annie at him, "don't you dare try to come down. You'd fall on top of me and we'd both be done for."

Sandy had decided the same thing and got his feet back on level ground. As much as he wanted to be with Annie to protect her, he could not manage a ladder. By this time Annie had reached the first level and was standing on the rock pathway. Another ladder went down to a lower level, but it was too dark to try to go farther without a lantern.

She looked around as far as she dared but didn't see anything very interesting. She had just put her foot on the ladder to start up when she heard voices in the shaft house above her.

"Golly, I don't dare let them see me," she said to herself. "They'd probably arrest me for trespassing."

She crouched down as far from the ladder as she could get, and hoped that the men would not come down, but their voices sounded closer and closer.

"I don't like this," one gruff voice said. "Where would a dog come from around here?"

"Oh, don't worry about him. Probably one of the village dogs up here hunting. That door was wide open. I suppose he just came in to look around."

"Well, I don't like it. It would be fine if we were caught here now after all our plans are made."

"Now listen here," the more cultivated voice commanded. "Who's bossing this job? I'm the one that does the worrying. All you have to do is follow directions."

"O.K., only I still don't like it."

The voices sounded right above Annie and a bright light shone down the shaft. Annie crept farther and farther back along the wall until at last she found a tiny niche where at one time or another someone had started to dig a passageway.

"If they turn in this direction I'm a goner," thought Annie.

She held her breath while the men started down the ladder.

"Careful on those steps, Ruff," said the cultivated

voice. "That ladder's almost as old as you are."

"They're O.K.," said the one called Ruff.

Annie saw him test his weight on the first two rungs, then less carefully step down the next few. Suddenly one of the rounds gave way. It had been strong enough for Annie's light weight, but under a heavier person it had broken. The lantern Ruff was carrying slid from his hand and crashed to the floor. The place was coal black. Annie could hear Ruff swearing under his breath.

"Are you all right, Ruff?" the voice at the top of the shaft asked.

"Yah, I grabbed the next round in time. Did you bring that other lantern with you?"

"I left it outside. Hold on there till I get it."

The voice died away. All Annie could hear was Ruff's heavy breathing. Then suddenly from the distance came a yelp of pain that could come only from Sandy. Annie started forward and then realized that she could not get past Ruff on the ladder. She retreated to her hiding place. Just in time, too, for a glow of light growing constantly brighter above at last was right over the shaft.

"That cur was out here again," said the man at the top of the shaft as he reached down to Ruff with the lantern.

"I told you that dog meant bad business," said Ruff.

"Don't be silly," returned his partner. "You can't blame a rotten ladder on a dog. Get going again and this time be careful. I'm coming down now."

Ruff quickly reached the first level and held the lantern up waiting for the other man. There was considerable grunting as the broken round was passed, but soon both were on safe ground.

Annie pushed herself as flat against the side of the niche as she could, but she did not have to worry, for the boss said, "There's the next ladder. Go on down."

Ruff started down very slowly, testing each step of the way. Soon he was out of sight, and the other followed him. The glow of the lantern and their voices came back to the place where Annie stood.

"What did you find out in town?"

"Some kind of interestin' things." Annie could tell Ruff was still on the ladder from the way he hesitated between words as he tested the next step. "I had to tell them who I was. No one recognized me."

"I suppose they greeted you with open arms? Prodigal son returned?"

"Huh, no one jumped out o' his shoes for joy!"

"I shouldn't think so. What did you tell them about me?"

"Just what you said. I'm your companion, bodyguard kinda. You were looking for a quiet place to write, so out of love for my home town I talked you into coming here."

"Haw, haw, and they fell for it?"

"Hook, line, and sinker."

"So far so good. What about the mine?"

"I didn't dare act too interested. The mine ain't been used for twenty years."

"Yes, yes, I know that. What else?"

"Well, it seems there was a cave-in down in the lower passageway. And a train robbery right below here the same night."

"So!"

"Well, that was twenty years ago. It makes a good story for the villagers now, but that's all."

"Let's hear the rest. That isn't all you found out, is it?"

"Let's see. There were two partners that owned the mine. One got a prison sentence—six years or so. Said he took the dough and fixed the books."

"What about the train robbery?"

"People thought it looked like him, but they couldn't find the money and no one could prove it."

"And the partner?"

"Heard he went off to S.A. to open a mine. No one knows where he is."

"That doesn't sound too bad, does it? Guess we can go ahead with our plans."

The light and the voices had both died away and Annie saw Sandy peering down at her from above.

"Gee, Sandy, did they hurt you? Boy, I didn't know we were going to get into anything like this. We're getting out of here before they come back."

She climbed the ladder as quickly as she could and headed for the door. As she rounded the corner of the cabin she discovered a car.

"Whew, a car! I didn't hear it! And there's a road. We just must have been half asleep, Sandy. That must go down to the train we heard this morning. Of course there had to be a road to haul the stuff out."

She examined the car, listening all the time for the voices of the men returning. It was a mammoth black sedan.

"Golly, one of them must have some dough," she whispered.

There was a piece of rope coiled up in the back seat, but otherwise there was nothing unusual about the car. It had a New York license plate but that told Annie nothing.

"We'd better get out of here before they come back," decided Annie, and she and Sandy started down the road. Looking ahead, however, Annie could see little place to hide if the car should start out before she was a long way from the mine.

"I guess we'll just have to wait until they go, Sandy. I hate to take the time because we've got to get to a town by night. We haven't anything but this one roll left to eat. I've got enough money to buy us a good supper if we get to a town, but I guess we'd be wise to keep out of sight until they go."

She scouted around until she found a comfortable place under some of the scrub pines, and they huddled there wishing the men would hurry. Sandy wanted to go exploring, but Annie held him tight, for as she told him, it would never do for the men to see him again. They would be sure to go hunting for whomever the dog was with.

Noon passed, and there was still no sign of the men. Annie pulled out the last roll, and girl and dog finished it, wishing they had some of the mountain stream water to go with it. Annie was disgusted that she had not gone down the road to begin with. Finally she made a bargain with herself.

"If they aren't out of there by the time the sun gets behind that lone pine on the other ridge, I'm going to start."

The sun crept nearer and nearer to the tree. Annie alternately worried about herself and about the men.

"Maybe the ladder broke and they're lying there hurt," she thought.

Then remembering the things the men had been talking about she wondered if they would find her and guess that she had overheard them. Really, she had no idea what they were up to, but it sounded as though something were going to happen.

"I wish something would happen right away," she

whispered to Sandy, and as if in answer to the wish, the two men appeared. They were talking to each other, but Annie was too far away to hear a word they said. They got into the car, and the leader, as though he were used to tight spots, turned the car around swiftly. It went down the steep road in a cloud of dust. As soon as the dust had settled Annie and Sandy followed the same road, for they were sure now that this road would lead them to civilization.

CHAPTER TWO

NEWCOMERS TO BUTTERNUT

The road they followed seemed to go on and on. Annie had expected to find that they were not far from the town or at least from the railroad, since it was from there that the ore must have been shipped. They walked for several miles before they saw far below them the railroad tracks like twin ribbons of silver at the bottom of the valley.

For a while the road stayed parallel with the tracks. Finally it turned toward them, and there below was a lovely little village. The mountains surrounded it completely, and with the sun behind the top of one of them the village was already in darkness, though the mountain top where Annie stood was still bright.

As she looked down the village lights began to go on here and there.

"Don't they look grand, Sandy? Just like homes should look—not all blacked out the way they are in Europe."

She fingered the lone quarter remaining in her pocket. Since she had promised Sandy a good supper she ought to go on down into the town. The village looked friendly, with its church steeple white against the deep night purple of the mountains. She was sure that down there their quarter would get them enough for the evening meal. But hungry and tired as she was, she still stood fascinated by the lights gradually winking on below them. Sandy watched her impatiently, anxious to get where there was food. It was not until a train whistled in the distance and then became visible below them that Annie started down.

The train chugged to a stop in the town. Then it came on out of the mountains and was lost to sight long before Annie reached the edge of town.

She followed what seemed to be the main street toward the center of the town. Every home seemed to blaze with lights, and in most of them families were sitting down to their evening meal. How she envied those children, not only their food, but their home, and most of all their parents.

"Even so, I'm luckier than some people—I've got Daddy Warbucks," she told herself. Still, he was a long way off, and she was suddenly very lonesome for him.

There were just a few homes not lighted. One of them, a big old place set back from the road, looked deserted. Annie thought she might be able to use it for the night. Without stopping to look at it she hurried on, anxious to find something for them to eat. Later there would be time enough to worry about a place to spend the night.

As she reached the shopping district she saw that here and there a store was still open. She passed several darkened shops and stopped before the first lighted one. It was not a restaurant nor a grocery. It was a shoe-repair shop. Bent over a work bench was a white-haired old man working on a shoe.

Ruefully Annie fingered the holes in her shoes. The pieces of blanket had not lasted long on the stony road. Apologetically she looked at Sandy.

"Could you go without supper tonight, Sandy? I know I promised you, but these soles are getting awfully hard to walk in."

Sandy looked gravely at the bedraggled soles and agreed with a small "arf."

Timidly Annie pushed open the door of the shop. The shoemaker looked up at her over the edge of his glasses.

"Well, you're coming in pretty late with your shoes. You ought to be home eating your supper."

He laid the shoe he was repairing on the table and came toward her.

"Why, you're new around here. I haven't seen you before, have I?"

"No, sir, I don't live around here. I was just going through town and I saw your light and my shoes are dreadfully thin on the bottom. Do you suppose—" She fished the quarter from her pocket and held it out. "Is this enough to fix them?"

The old man looked carefully at the quarter and then at Annie.

"Of course. That's plenty. Take them off and I'll fix them in a jiffy."

He pulled a bench out for her and wearily she sat down and unfastened the shoes.

"Whew!" whistled the shoeman as he took the shoes from her. "These shoes have seen a lot of wear, young lady. They need new soles all right."

"Is that more than a quarter? I—I can't pay any more than that."

"A quarter will just do it—but how about your dog's feet? Aren't they going to need some repair work, too?"

Annie laughed and Sandy wagged his tail to show that he was still feeling pretty good. He sat down close to the shoemaker to watch him work on Annie's shoes.

"I wish I had feet like Sandy's," said Annie. "His never seem to wear out. I tried going barefoot to save shoe leather, but those mountain roads are too stony for me."

She rubbed her feet to see if she could get some of the soreness out.

"You aren't planning to go any farther tonight, are you?" questioned the shoemaker.

"Oh, no," Annie assured him. "We just came down

to town to find something to eat and then we'll look for a place to sleep."

"Do you mean to say you haven't had anything to eat yet? Well, I can tell you what we're going to do about that. You're coming home with me just as soon as I finish your shoes."

"Oh, no, we couldn't do that," exclaimed Annie. "You've done enough for us already. Why, I'll bet it costs a lot more than a quarter to fix those soles."

The shoemaker looked over his glasses at her.

"How much money have you got in that pocket?"

Annie couldn't meet his eyes.

"I thought so. Not a cent, is there? And I suppose you'd rather starve and let that dog of yours starve before you'd let anyone help you. You're coming home with me. You there, what's your name, Sandy, you could use a bowl of milk and maybe a good big bone, couldn't you?"

Excited at the idea of a bone, Sandy ran around the little shop barking as loudly as he could. Annie couldn't help laughing at him, and finally she had to give in.

"All right, but I hate to think of troubling you."

"Trouble me, young lady! Why I'm so lonesome over in my house I think I'd almost be willing to get a porcupine down from the mountains for company. And just today I put a big pot of beans in my oven to bake. I thought I'd never eat them all, but I got a hankerin' for them and they're no good if you bake just enough for one person. So you see, some one must have told me I'd have company tonight."

He finished Annie's shoes and while she was putting them on he got out a neat blue overcoat from the closet at the back of the store. He turned out the lights and locked the front door. They walked back the same way Annie and Sandy had come in to town, past the lighted houses she had envied, past the deserted house she had noticed. Almost at the edge of town he turned up a path to a neat little white house. It was too dark to tell much about it at night except that there were beds of sweet-smelling flowers somewhere nearby.

He opened the door and Annie was amazed to see that it had not been locked.

The shoemaker saw her surprise and laughed. "Why, we never lock our houses here in Butternut. I do lock my store and everyone in the neighborhood laughs at me for doing it, but there's nothing here at home that anyone would want."

Annie disagreed with him when he had turned on the light, for everything in the house seemed to have been chosen with care. Annie would have been glad to have any of it. It was a man's house, there was no doubting that. In the living room was a big fireplace with a leather chair in front of it. One wall was covered with bookcases all filled to overflowing with

Annie, Boot and Sandy Walked up the Path

beautifully bound books. There were a table and two chairs in the room too, but they looked as if they were seldom used. It was the leather chair that got all the wear.

Annie followed the shoemaker out to the kitchen. Going through the dining room she saw that it too had had little or no use. Out in the kitchen everything was spotless. There was a white metal table with two chairs next to it, an enameled stove, and a refrigerator. Up above were rows of cupboards. The shoemaker opened one of the cupboards and took out two plates and glasses. From the table drawer he took the silverware. All the time he was busy setting the table, Annie was just as busy sniffing at the wonderful smells from the oven.

Finally everything was ready and the round brown pot of beans came out. Annie thought of the can of beans she had had the night before, and discovered that a "can" of something that had sounded so good last night couldn't hold a candle to something home-cooked.

The shoemaker piled Annie's plate high and ordered her to start eating while he got something for Sandy. He didn't bother her with questions until she had pushed her plate away from her and sat back contented.

"Now, I've got a spare room upstairs that's never been used. I don't know why I fixed it up, for I've been here ten years and the bed hasn't been slept in once. From the looks of you you could do with a rest for a few days. You can't keep on going forever, you know."

"Gee, that's swell, but I can't just take something from you that way. I can't pay you back—"

"Pay me back! If you knew how much I wanted company around here! The people of the village are friendly enough, but unless you were born and raised here they pretty much let you go your own way. Why, I'm the newest person in town, and I've been here ten years."

"Golly, I didn't know there were really places like this. Doesn't anything ever change here?"

"Well, it will be something of a shock to the village when they find you here. I'm afraid they'll kind of wonder where you came from. You know everyone has to know every single thing that goes on. When there aren't many people to talk about you have to know a lot about each one to keep the conversation going."

Annie looked worried.

"I don't think I ought to stay. I'll get you into trouble. I know what a lot of gossip can do to anyone. Sandy and I had better clear out before the village wakes up tomorrow."

"You'll do nothing of the kind. What the village can say about us can't harm us, and besides they need something to wake them up a little bit. Of course, if you don't mind stretching the truth a little bit, it would be easier if you'd call me Uncle Jack and we could tell them you'd come to visit me for a while."

"Oh, I'd love to have an uncle. I've never had any real family, except Daddy Warbucks who isn't actually my own daddy either. I keep wishing I had loads and loads of relatives, but wishing doesn't do any good."

Uncle Jack, seeing that Annie was as lonesome for affection as he himself was, vowed that he would keep her with him as long as he could. Annie too, though she had known him just a few hours, felt that Uncle Jack was an old friend. By bedtime she had told him a great deal about Daddy and about all her adventures since Daddy had left. This recital only made Jack more sure that he wanted to keep the brave youngster with him. Realizing, though, that she would be too proud to accept his home without repaying him, he decided not to say anything more about her staying until he thought of some plan by which she would feel he needed her. Little did he realize how badly he would need her in the next few weeks. .

Finally Annie was too sleepy to talk any more, and Jack carried the drowsy girl up to the spick-and-span room.

Annie was awakened the next morning by the sun shining in her eyes as it had the day before, but this time the sunbeam didn't come through a hole in a dirty roof. It came through the shining pane of the bedroom window. She sat up and blinked. She couldn't remember coming upstairs at all, and the dainty room made her feel that she was still dreaming. Looking down, she saw Sandy yawning up at her. Suddenly remembering where she was she tumbled out of bed and started dressing.

"Golly, Sandy, isn't this wonderful? I don't know what we can do to pay Uncle Jack back, but at least maybe I can go down and get breakfast for him. Come on, but be quiet so we don't wake him up."

Quietly the two tiptoed downstairs, but long before she reached the kitchen door Annie found that Uncle Jack was up before her. There was a wonderful smell of pancakes and sausage coming from the kitchen.

"Boy, oh boy, is this different from yesterday morning," exclaimed Annie, stopping in the doorway.

Uncle Jack, busy turning a pancake, looked over his shoulder at her.

"Good morning, Annie. Why different from yesterday?"

"Well, all we had for breakfast yesterday was half an old roll and we'd slept in an old miners' shack up in the mountains."

Uncle Jack seemed to freeze, with a pancake raised in midair. His face paled. Annie, thinking there was some superstition about the camp being haunted, reassured him.

"Oh, it wasn't bad, kind of fallen in in spots, and dusty, but at least it was some protection."

Uncle Jack had recovered his composure.

"But that place hasn't been used for twenty years. You might have fallen through those rotten timbers and hurt yourself."

"Oh, we were careful, and besides, the floor seemed solid. It was the roof that wasn't any too good."

Seeing that the mention of the mine disturbed him, Annie changed the subject without telling him about the men she had seen there.

"What can I do to help, Uncle Jack?"

"Nothing except fall to and eat some of those pancakes. I've had my breakfast already."

"But I want to help. Let me do the dishes then."

"All right. I've got to be down at the store soon. You can clean up the kitchen and then come down to my shop if you want to help."

When Uncle Jack left, Annie was eating "just one more" pancake, but as soon as he was out the door she hustled around, doing dishes, making beds, dusting and sweeping till the little house shone.

"I'd like to make a pie for Uncle Jack," she told Sandy, "but he told us to come down to the store so

I'd better leave that till later."

She looked around once again to see if everything was in order. Then together girl and dog left the house.

"Doesn't it seem queer not to lock the door?" marveled Annie as she closed it behind her. "Why, most places I've been in you had to lock up even if you were just going across the hall. To think we've still got places where there isn't any crime! Do you know, Sandy, evidently that train robbery those fellows were talking about was the only bad thing that's happened here in twenty years if they're still talking about it. No wonder they have to find out about everyone in town to have something to talk about."

The road down to the town was beginning to take on a familiar aspect to Annie. She was interested to see that the houses she had admired the night before looked just as good in the daylight. She watched for the deserted house of the night before, and as she came toward it she discovered a car parked out in front.

"Golly, Sandy, that's the car from the mine! Boy, I hope we don't see those fellows."

But that was too much to hope for. Just as she reached the sidewalk to the house Ruff and his boss and a third man came out of the door.

The third man was saying, "It hasn't been used for a long time, but it's a well-built house, and it won't take much fixing up. I can have it ready in a week."

"And you're sure there won't be much noise around? I won't be bothered? I can't write unless I have quiet."

"You needn't worry about that, Mr. Halk. That's one thing we don't have much of in Butternut—noise."

"All right, I'll take it for six months and if it proves satisfactory I might be interested in buying it. Probably would do me good to get away from the city when I wanted to work."

"Oh, I'm sure you'll like it here, Mr. Halk," beamed the salesman. "Nice friendly people."

"Not too friendly I hope," laughed Mr. Halk. "I came here to work, not to be entertained."

Ruff had said not a word. Annie on the sidewalk had been walking slowly to hear what was going on. Her curiosity overcame her fear of the men, and besides, she thought, the men hadn't seen her at the mine, so what difference did it make? She had forgotten Sandy though. She saw Ruff nudge Mr. Halk and motion toward Sandy. Halk recognized Sandy too, but he shook his head warningly at Ruff and turned back to the salesman.

"I'll stay at the hotel till it's ready. But get at it right away. I want to settle down to work." Annie didn't dare hurry or show in any way that she recognized these two. Though everything in her wanted her to run, she kept on at the same leisurely pace, keeping one hand on Sandy. She could feel his hair bristling as it did when he was mad, but she held tight to him so that he couldn't go for Mr. Halk.

As soon as she was out of their sight she breathed a sigh of relief. "Whew, that was a close call, Sandy. You've got to be awful careful not to tangle with them. I can't figure out what they're up to, but I'll bet it's no good.

"Maybe I should tell Uncle Jack about this," she thought. "If those fellows are up to something, the town ought to be warned about it. Only I haven't any real proof. They had as much right up there at the mine as I did. I guess I'd better keep quiet until I know more about them."

She had no trouble finding the little shoe-repair shop with it's big letters, "Jack Boot" on the window. Uncle Jack was busy polishing a pile of shoes as Annie came in.

"Can't I do that, Uncle Jack?" she wanted to know.

"Why, I don't see why not, only you'll probably get your hands stained."

"Huh, what's a little stain, and besides it's fun to make dull things turn bright. That's why dusting and washing windows are so much fun. And it's the same way—," she stopped to roll up her sleeves and don a leather apron several sizes too big for her that Jack handed to her. "That's the way people are. They seem so dull when you first meet them, and then you talk to them for a while and they start to sparkle just the way the shoes do."

"Yes, but there are some that work the other way, Annie," Jack reminded her. "They sparkle and shine when you first see them, but when you get to know them their polish is all worn off."

"I know," said Annie, "but I think there are more of my kind than of the other."

"I hope you're right."

"Well, I've seen lots of people wandering around this way, and most all of them turned out to be good people. O' course there are some of the others, but they just make the good ones seem better than ever."

"All you've seen though is a short glance, Annie. I'm afraid all your people wouldn't be so nice when you get to know them."

"I don't know." Annie wondered at Jack's outlook. "I think you can tell what a person's like by the little things he does as well as the big things. If he's good in little things he's got to be good in big things too. Now you, I know you couldn't do anything bad. It just wouldn't be in you."

"Why, thank you, Annie, but you may be disappointed. You've only known me a day. For all you know I may be the worst kind of criminal."

"Go on," laughed Annie, "nobody could make me believe you ever did anything wrong."

Before Jack could reply the door opened and two

of the village women came in. One of them had a
pair of shoes under her arm, but you could see they
had something much more important to talk about
than their shoes.

"Have you seen Mr. Halk yet, Jack?"

"Mr. Halk, who's he?" questioned the shoemaker.

"Why you know, the famous writer." Annie
guessed that Mr. Halk's tale of being an author had
been greatly exaggerated, but the women were too
excited about having a celebrity in Butternut to
question it.

"He's going to stay here. In the old Burn house."

Uncle Jack started in surprise, but it wasn't necessary to ask questions to get the story from the women.
Interrupting each other they told everything they
knew, and probably a little more than they knew,
about the newcomer.

"You remember Ruff?"

"You know that good-for-nothing son of Mary
Ruff?"

"But, of course, Matilda, Jack's new here. He
wouldn't remember about it. It must be fifteen years
ago that he left, Jack. He never did a tap of work
anyway, and finally he ran off with the little money
Mary had saved."

"Well, he's back! And you can't guess what he's
doing."

"He's bodyguard for H. Huntingdon Halk."

"And when Mr. Halk wanted a quiet place to write, Ruff told him about Butternut. Imagine him remembering it all these years! I couldn't believe it."

"Hum," Uncle Jack seemed skeptical. "Ruff couldn't expect much of a welcome after the way he went off."

"Oh, but he's changed now," one of the women defended him. "If he's with such a polished man as Mr. Halk he's bound to have changed."

"Yes, and remember what a loud talker and bully he used to be? Why now he hardly says a word. All the time Mr. Halk was talking to us, he just stood there and smiled—the friendliest sort of smile."

"Oh, by the way," Uncle Jack interrupted them, "you haven't met my niece, Annie Warbucks. Annie, this is Mrs. Bolker and Mrs. Speedle."

One of the women gave Annie a nod and the other a "glad to know you," but they were so busy thinking of Mr. Halk that all the worrying Annie had done about the excitement she would cause had been unnecessary.

"Do you suppose we could give a party for him? Maybe a literary tea. That's the stylish thing in New York, I understand," said Mrs. Speedle.

"Oh, that would be grand. If we can only get our plans made before Mrs. Bart plans something."

"We could have—"

They started out the door, their heads close to-

The Two Women Talked Excitedly

gether over their planning. Uncle Jack remembered
that Mrs. Speedle had had shoes under her arm, and
he went out to call to her, but they were talking so
fast and so hard that they didn't hear him.

"Well, she'll just have to make herself another trip,
I guess," he told Annie.

"Mr. Halk certainly did us a service," he commented. "Those two are the worst gossips in town,
and if they were too busy to pay any attention to you,
no one else is going to question your being here. It
looks as though we wouldn't have to do any explaining."

"I'd rather do the explaining, Uncle Jack, than have
that fellow in town. I don't like him."

"Why Annie, do you know him?"

"Oh, no, I don't know him." Annie thought of telling Jack about the mine, and again she changed her
mind. "But he and that Ruff and another fellow, a
real-estate man, I guess, were coming out of that
closed-up house that sits way back in the yard."

"That's the Burn place."

"Well, they were just coming out of there when I
was coming down to the store. Mr. Halk said he'd
rent it for six months and then if he liked it he'd buy
it."

"I can't see any reason to dislike him for that,"
Uncle Jack commented. "That house has stood empty
a long time. The town will be glad to have someone

in it."

"Well, maybe, and I suppose the women will like him too. He's good-looking—tall, with white hair and a tiny white mustache. Oh, he's smooth all right. I guess that's what I didn't like about him—he's too smooth—he's oily."

Uncle Jack laughed at her, but she still insisted. "I'll bet you dollars to doughnuts he causes plenty of excitement around here before his six months are up."

"That's no bet. Look at all the excitement he's caused already."

"I don't mean that kind. There's going to be trouble around here before he leaves. I'm sure of it."

CHAPTER THREE

In the next two or three days Annie was surer than ever that Mr. Halk was in Butternut for no good.

"For a writer," she told Sandy, "he certainly spends a lot of time visiting."

And that was true. He had said he wanted peace and quiet, but he spent most of his time wandering around the village, talking to everyone he met. Annie encountered him his second day in the town. He was especially interested in Sandy, and Annie, seeing what he was up to, told him the things that would make him feel most sure of himself.

"That's a grand dog you've got there," he told her. "A dog is a grand companion if you have one that stays with you as yours seems to. I have noticed you several times in the past day, and you've never been alone. He's always been with you."

"Oh," said Annie, "once in a while he goes off on his own. He did just the other day, and when he got home he was so tired he wouldn't even eat."

"Where do you suppose he went?" asked Mr. Halk, relief showing in his eyes.

"Oh, probably up in the hills. There are rabbits

54

to chase and lots of places to explore."

Annie could feel Halk grow more and more sure of himself. He must have decided that no one had found out his secret. It was more than Annie could take and she decided to let him do a little worrying at least.

"I should go up some day with him. I want to explore, myself. I've always wanted to go way down in the old mine. Some day I'll have to take him up there. It's fun climbing around in the hills. Do you ever go exploring, Mr. Halk?"

Mr. Halk looked at her questioningly and then decided that her face was innocent of any knowledge of the mine. He regained his friendly attitude.

"Ho, ho, Annie, I'm afraid my exploring days are over. I'm getting to be an old man now."

"Why, I'll bet you could take these mountains with the best of them," soft-soaped Annie. "And I know you can climb ladders even if you grunt doing it," she added to herself.

"He sure is trying to find out everything about us," she told Sandy. "We'd better steer clear of them if we can—you especially. You don't want to get in Halk's way again, and Ruff didn't sound as though he liked you very well either."

Ruff, as Uncle Jack had predicted, was no favorite in the village. Even though he worked for Mr. Halk people didn't forget what he had been like. Though he did very little talking now, people didn't like the look in his eyes. Even Mrs. Speedle, who had insisted the first day that he had changed his ways, admitted that the way he stared at anyone "fair gave her the creeps." The townspeople accepted him just as long as he could tell them more about H. Huntingdon Halk, but when everyone had milked him dry of all he knew, or rather of all he would tell, they ignored him. He held a queer position with Halk, for though supposedly a servant the two seemed to hold very confidential conversations that didn't look at all like a master giving a servant directions.

After the first couple of days, after the people had found out all they could and had pretty much forgotten about him, he was seldom seen around town. Annie noticed it but no one else seemed to think it was important. Early in the morning he would take the big car and go off toward the hills. He didn't reappear till late in the afternoon.

But Halk was always in evidence. He sat in the hotel lobby and visited with all who came in. He almost held court, for everyone who could think of any possible excuse to be there came to see the celebrity. Annie would have been interested to know that many of his conversations led around to the old mine and the train robbery. The townspeople thought nothing of it. There was certainly nothing very exciting to talk to a stranger about and this was one thing that would interest him.

Annie remembered the story Ruff had told about the mine, but try as she would she couldn't put what she knew together with either Ruff or Halk. It bothered her, for she was sure there was something more to it than she knew. Finally she made up her mind to stop worrying about it until she got some other facts to go with what she already knew.

She did get her facts, and all too soon. As anxious as she had been to find out more about the mine, when she knew what had really happened she wished she had never heard about it.

Each morning when Uncle Jack went down to open the store, Annie stayed home to straighten up the house. The day after she had talked to Mr. Halk she decided to do more than just dust and sweep and make beds.

"I'm going to start on housecleaning," she told Sandy.

Sandy wasn't very enthusiastic about it. He curled up out in the kitchen, out of the way of broom and mop and dustcloth.

Annie started in with a will.

"I guess those books had better come out first. I'll start at the top of the bookcase and dust each one."

She found a stepladder and climbed up to the top step. She sat down and started pulling each book out of its place, giving it a thorough dusting and then putting it back. She enjoyed handling the beautiful books. Uncle Jack had told her he had put the bindings on them himself. It was a good pastime for long winter evenings. She looked carefully at each volume, admiring the workmanship. When one looked especially interesting she glanced through it to see the pictures. It took her a long time to finish one shelf since she stopped so long over each book.

As she slid down a step to start on the second shelf she glanced at the clock. "Leapin' lizards!" she wailed. "Look at the time. I've got to hurry if I want to get this done before time to get lunch."

She hurried through the next few volumes, not even glancing at their titles. "I'll come back and look at them as soon as I have some time," she promised herself. "I could read some of them evenings."

Suddenly she found a most unusual book. Books are heavy things, but this one was so light when she picked it up that she almost let it drop from surprise. It was so queer she couldn't resist peeking inside. She opened the cover and, to her amazement, found not a book, but a box full of newspaper clippings. She scrambled down the ladder and sat on the floor to investigate. It never occurred to her that this might be something she ought not look at.

The top clipping was one about the twenty-year-old train robbery. Annie read it through. She had been looking for more about the robbery and here it was, literally right in her lap.

There was little enough about the robbery even now. The train had been stopped just north of the village. That would be the place where the mountains closed in on both sides, the place where Annie had first seen it from up above. There had been a big gold shipment in the express car and evidently the robbers had known it. That was all the first article told her.

She glanced through the pile to find another headline about the robbery, but didn't see any, so she started back at the second clipping to find what else was there. This one gave an account of the cave-in at the mine. Evidently the robbery had made the edition before this one. This article mentioned Horace Gila and James Burn, partners in the mine.

"Gee, that must be the Burn that owned that old home," thought Annie.

Sandy, hearing no sounds of housecleaning coming from the living-room, poked his nose around the dining-room door. Seeing Annie sitting on the floor he ventured over to investigate.

Annie jumped as his black nose appeared over her shoulder. She laughed and went back to her reading.

"How do you suppose so many things could happen at one time, Sandy?" she asked. "A train robbery, a cave-in, and here's talk about bankruptcy at the mine. More things happened in one day than happen in a big city in a week, and then nothing else happens for twenty years. I guess there's something to that saying 'It never rains but it pours.' "

She folded up the second clipping and turned to the next one. At the top of it was a picture of a young man with dark hair. She looked at it for a moment, a puzzled expression on her face, and then cried, "Sandy, it's Uncle Jack!"

And it was! He had no mustache then and his hair was not white, but there could be little doubt about it—it was Uncle Jack.

Anxious to know what the clipping told about him she read on. His name according to the article was not Jack Boot, but James Burn—one of the partners in the mine. The headlines read "OWNER OF BURN'S MINE ARRESTED."

"Oh, golly, Sandy, poor Uncle Jack," moaned Annie, but bravely she read on, wanting to know the rest of it.

It was certainly not a pretty story. The evidence was all against him. The cave-in had injured several men and an investigation had been started immediately. When the records for the mine were examined, the auditors discovered that the accounts had been neatly juggled. The mine was virtually bankrupt. James Burn was acting as treasurer and all blame was laid at his feet. Even his partner, Horace Gila, had accused him.

Article after article appeared following the trial, for it had been sensational enough to break into front page on all the city papers as well as the Butternut Daily. Though no bank accounts could be found which contained the missing money, all the evidence pointed toward James Burn. After what seemed according to the clippings to be a long-drawn-out trial in which Horace Gila was the main witness, James Burn was sentenced to six years.

"Oh, Sandy," sobbed Annie, putting her head against Sandy's furry neck, "it can't be true. I know Uncle Jack would never do a thing like that."

But it seemed true enough. There were more clippings and a final picture of him, flanked on both sides by police, as he was forced to pose for the photographers just before boarding the train which would take him to the penitentiary. There was one last item —a tiny clipping saying that the mine would no longer be operated and that Horace Gila was leaving to take a position in South America.

"I don't care what the papers say, I know Uncle Jack couldn't do a thing like that."

Annie couldn't help worrying though, and she went over the clippings again and again in hopes of finding some clue to James Burn's innocence. Disappointed, she gathered up the clippings at last, and put them back in their box. Drying her tears she tried to decide what to do next.

"I can't let Uncle Jack know I've seen them. If I tell him I've been cleaning the bookcase he'll guess. I'd better try to get them back just as I found them and leave the bookcases alone."

She climbed back up the ladder and set the book back carefully, evening the row so that it did not look as though it had been disturbed. She lugged the stepladder back in its place so that Uncle Jack would not ask what she had been doing with it.

"There," she told herself, looking at the shelves, "everything is just the way it was."

She was not a moment too soon, for just then Uncle Jack called to her from the front door.

"Annie, are you all right?"

Annie hastened to meet him. "Why, of course, Uncle Jack. Why?"

"Here it is noon, and usually you're down to the shop by ten. I worried about you."

"Oh, noon! I'm sorry I worried you and I haven't even got lunch yet."

"Don't worry. We can open a can of soup. I just thought something might have happened to you. What were you doing all morning that kept you so busy?"

Annie thought fast for an answer. She knew it would have to be a fib, and she hated that, but she couldn't tell him the truth.

"Why, I don't know where the time went. I played

Annie Read the Clippings Again and Again

with Sandy and dusted and swept, and that's all. I can't see where the time went."

Jack looked at her puzzled. This didn't sound like Annie. He had wanted her to play, to forget about working and just be a little girl, but Annie was so used to responsibility that she was uncomfortable unless she were really working. Now to have her admit that she had spent a whole morning without accomplishing a thing didn't sound right. She seemed upset, too, and Jack was afraid she would think he was scolding her if he said anything more about it. He started off on a new track, told her what had happened at the store, who had been in, and what little news they had brought with them.

Annie hurried to get the lunch ready, and she listened with little comment. Her mind was awhirl with the staggering news she had, and she was afraid she would say something about it without meaning to. She did not dare meet Uncle Jack's eyes, and sensing the strain she was under he worried as much about her as she was worrying about him.

Finally lunch was ready and they sat down. Annie made a pretense of eating, but it was difficult to swallow anything.

"Did you know that Mrs. Speedle and Mrs. Bolker are giving that party for Mr. Halk—that literary tea they were talking about? All the élite have been invited."

"Did you get an invitation?"

"Of course not. The 'élite' here are the ones whose grandfathers drove the Indians out. I'm just a new-comer, a nobody."

"Well, so is Halk."

"But he's an exhibit—a curiosity. That's why he's so popular."

"I'll bet he loses his popularity before long," said Annie, thinking of his connection with the mine and her feeling that he was here on questionable business.

"I wouldn't have known about the party only Mrs. Bart, the bank president's wife, and Mrs. Cutler were in at the same time. They couldn't talk about anything else. Mrs. Bart didn't seem too enthusiastic about it, but of course she wouldn't unless she were at the head of it."

"Well, if Halk is really used to society, I bet he gets a laugh out of this hick stuff," commented Annie.

"Oh, yes, there is some other news, too," said Uncle Jack. "The whole town's mad at Miss Jens."

"Miss Jens? That's the little librarian, isn't it? Why?"

"Well, everyone wants a copy of Halk's book to read. Miss Jens hasn't any, and she says none of the places she orders books ever heard of him. Mrs. Bart was furious. She said she'd never go near the library again, that she'd go down to Raymont where there's a good library."

"Didn't I tell you," crowed Annie. "I'll bet he never did write a book. I'll bet that's just an excuse for being here."

"The townspeople don't feel that way, Annie. They think he's wonderful. You'd better be careful how you talk about him to anyone else."

"Oh, sure, I'll be careful, but I'll bet if I'd come here and told them I danced before the King of England they'd believe me. The trouble with them is they never have a chance to see celebrities around here."

"Well," said Uncle Jack, "I'd at least like to see the celebrity who's causing all this commotion."

"Haven't you seen him, Uncle Jack? For gosh sakes, where have you been? He's all over town it seems to me."

"He hasn't been near my shoe store yet," returned Jack.

"Well," consoled Annie, "to my way of thinking you haven't missed much."

"I really should stop at the hotel some time and get a look at him. That's where he holds his court, I understand."

"That's right, and he'd probably 'love' to talk to you. I heard Mrs. Speedle tell Mrs. Bolker that he thought everything in Butternut was simply charming."

"Whew," laughed Uncle Jack. "If those were his exact words, I don't know whether I want to meet him or not.

"Are you coming down to the shop this afternoon?" he asked, changing the subject.

"I don't think so, Uncle Jack. I've got some things I want to do."

"Annie, are you sure you feel all right?" Jack was worried.

"Why sure. If you really want me down there for something I'll come. I just thought—."

"Oh, it's all right, Annie. Goodness knows I don't need you there. With everyone interested in nothing but Mr. Halk and the party, they're all talking new clothes, not bringing in old things to repair. You do whatever you want to."

"Well, maybe I'll be down later, Uncle Jack."

Jack was still puzzled and worried about her when he left for the shop.

"I hate to have him worry about me," thought Annie, "but I've just got to have some time to do some figuring."

She stacked the dishes in the sink and left them. If Jack had seen that he would have been still more worried, for it was not like Annie to leave housekeeping jobs undone. But she was too worried to think about them. She settled herself in Jack's comfortable leather chair and tried to fit the pieces of this puzzle together.

"Uncle Jack *is* James Burn all right and he did serve

that prison sentence, I'm sure, but I don't believe he was guilty. I'd like to know what happened to that Horace Gila, and something more about that train robbery. Seems to me those two must be connected some way. And then there's the cave-in. Maybe that wasn't an accident either. Boy, there are so many things I don't know, and I've just got to find out.

"There's this Halk, too. He must be interested in that mine or he wouldn't have gone up there his first day in town."

The problem seemed to have so many different parts, and no two of them would fit together. It was like having a jigsaw puzzle with half the pieces missing.

"I suppose I shouldn't worry about it, just forget it, but somehow I feel as though I ought to know all about it. It's as though I knew something would happen and I ought to be ready for it when it comes. The only thing I know of is to start asking questions around town and see if I can find out more about it."

But that too was more easily talked about than done, for Annie was with Jack most of the time and she couldn't ask questions while he was there, or he'd guess that somehow she had found out his secret. Finally, after a great deal of figuring, she found what she thought was a foolproof idea.

Pleased with herself and anxious to put her plan into action she hurried down to the shoe shop. Luck

ter for Jack was alone, and in great excite-
nie greeted him with, "Uncle Jack, I've got
idea!"

She acted so much more like herself that Jack couldn't help but laugh to think of all the worrying he had done.

"What are you going to do? Revolutionize the shoe business or housekeeping?"

"Well, I'm going to try to revolutionize," Annie stumbled over the big word, "your shoe business. Why don't we start a delivery service?"

"A delivery service!"

"Sure," Annie explained, "people don't like lugging a pair of shoes around, and I could pick them up one day and take them back the next. That would be twenty-four-hour service. When they bring their shoes in, sometimes they don't get down for them for almost a week."

"Maybe that's not such a bad idea, Annie," Uncle Jack praised her, "but it would mean a lot of work for you."

"Pooh, that's no work. It would be fun going to everyone's house and talking them into getting more repairing done."

"All right, if you want to try it, it's O.K. with me, but if you get tired, you stop. Don't work too hard at it."

"That's not going to be work, Uncle Jack. It'll be

like playing a game."

Annie was triumphant at having an excus[e]
the villagers so easily. She knew that she could
some way of talking about the old mine, and she was
sure that somewhere among the villagers there would
be someone who could add pieces to her puzzle.

Bright and early the next morning she started out,
the big basket Uncle Jack had given her over her
arm and Sandy romping around her.

"Sandy, we're not going out for fun. This is serious
business," she scolded. "If you can't behave yourself
I'll let you stay with Uncle Jack next time."

Sandy did not seem very worried at the threat. He
still thought this was some new kind of adventure,
and, in a way, it was. It was not as easy, however, as
she thought it would be, for often children came to
the door, or the grown-ups were too busy to stop
to visit. Though her basket filled with shoes, she
found out nothing at all about the mine mystery. She
was pretty discouraged as she lugged the heavy
basket back to the shoe store.

"But I won't give up," she told Sandy. "It's sticking at a thing that counts. Maybe it will take a long
time, but I still think that I can learn more this way
than any other way."

Uncle Jack was surprised and pleased at the number of pairs of shoes she had.

"I'll get right to work at them so they'll be ready for you to deliver tomorrow," he told her. "Why don't you take the rest of the day off now?"

"Oh, not yet, I can make another trip before time to get dinner. I'll just finish up the houses on the north end of town before I call it a day."

Glowing with Uncle Jack's praise, she started out once more, sure that this time she would find not only shoes, but also what she was hunting for.

One of the first houses she stopped at was Mrs. Speedle's. Mrs. Speedle had been the one Annie had met her first day at Jack's store, and since then she had found that Mrs. Speedle really was the worst gossip in town. She would rather talk than eat. When she kept quiet long enough to hear all the things she knew about the village, no one knew, but there was no person better informed as to the comings and goings, the family skeletons, and the scandals in the neighborhood than Mrs. Speedle.

"If anyone can help me," thought Annie, "she can. I don't see why I didn't think of her before."

Mrs. Speedle herself came to the door in answer to Annie's knock, but she had no shoes to give Annie.

"Golly," thought Annie, "I've got to have some excuse to get in. I can't pass up this chance."

Aloud she asked, "Do you suppose I could have a glass of water, Mrs. Speedle? I hate to trouble you, but I'm so thirsty!"

"Why, of course, Annie, come on in, but don't you bring that dog in here. I just washed the kitchen floor."

"Oh no, I wouldn't bring Sandy into a house, Mrs. Speedle." Annie followed her inside, leaving Sandy looking desolately through the screen door. Other times she would have felt sorry leaving him behind, but she had too much on her mind for it to bother her.

Mrs. Speedle poured her a big glass of water from a jug in her ice box. Annie sipped it slowly, wanting to have as much time as possible to visit.

"Boy, this is nice and cold! It's as cold as that mountain spring up by the old miners' cabin."

"Have you been up there?" asked Mrs. Speedle, as Annie had hoped her would.

"Oh sure, that's the most exciting place around here, isn't it?"

"Well, I suppose so, in a spooky sort of way. I don't think I'd want a youngster of mine playing up there."

"What's spooky about it?" Annie probed.

"Well, you know, that James Burn, the one that used to live in that big house that Mr. Halk has taken, stole all the money from the company."

"Oh, sure," Annie thought she might as well admit that. "But I can't see anything very spooky about that."

Mrs. Speedle, to make her story more exciting,

almost whispered, "But everything happened all at once. The train robbery and the cave-in all the same day. People say that the train robbers were hiding in that section of the mine and that Burn planned the cave-in to get rid of the lot of them. That way he could have all the money."

"Oh, was Burn one of the robbers, too?"

"That's what people think, but no one ever could prove it. They never found any of the money. You know it's funny how we got talking about this. That's what Mr. Halk and I were talking about too."

"Why do you suppose Mr. Halk would be interested in that," wondered Annie.

"Why it's for his new novel, he said. Just think, Butternut in a book!" she marveled.

"I hope he tells nice things about it," Annie said.

"My goodness, Annie, there's nothing bad to tell about except James Burn and he's not part of Butternut anymore, and maybe Ruff, but Ruff's Halk's man so he wouldn't be apt to talk about him. Goodness, Mr. Halk's too nice to do anything like that anyway! What ever put that idea in your head!"

It looked to Annie as if her fountain of new information had run dry, so she thanked her for the water and left, feeling that her afternoon had not been entirely wasted.

"I couldn't help but give that woman a little bit to worry about," Annie confided in Sandy. "I never saw a woman that could talk as much as she can.

"I still am not very far ahead on my problem though. If I could find out why Halk is so interested in that mine I think the whole thing would clear up. He holds the key to the whole business, I bet."

CHAPTER FOUR

THE BOOK-BOX BECOMES IMPORTANT

When Annie reached the store she realized her basket was still empty.

"Golly, Uncle Jack will think that's funny. After all I got the first trip, he'll think it's queer I didn't get any the second time."

She considered going back to some of the houses she hadn't tried, but it was too late for that.

"I guess I'll just have to tell him the truth," she decided, but added, "only I don't have to tell him what we were talking about."

Uncle Jack was cleaning up for the night. He had finished some of the shoes Annie had brought, but a pile of them still lay on the floor where Annie had dumped them.

"I didn't do so well this time, Uncle Jack." Annie thought it wise to tell him so before he asked her.

"Well, I'm rather glad. You did too well on that first trip. I'll have all I can do to get that pile ready for you to deliver tomorrow. Where did you go this time?"

"I started at Mrs. Speedle's and stopped there too."

Jack laughed. "You ought to have known you

wouldn't get very far if you went there. Did she have any new gossip?"

"Well, not very much," Annie hesitated. "She did say that Mr. Halk was going to use Butternut for his next novel."

"I'd like to see the faces of some of Butternut's leading citizens when the thing's published," laughed Jack. "I'll bet he doesn't treat them too gently."

"That's what I warned Mrs. Speedle, but she is sure that no one in town has a thing to hide, and she ought to know." Annie was sorry she had said that, for after all, wasn't Uncle Jack hiding something? She hastened to add, "As for me, I'm still betting that he never wrote a book and doesn't have any intentions of writing one."

As she talked she glanced out of the window and noticed a tall figure coming down the street.

"Hey, Uncle Jack. Look, here he comes now. I'll bet he's coming here!"

"Well, well, I won't have to go hunting him then, will I? So I'm going to get a glimpse of the great man!"

The late afternoon light was kind to Halk. He looked younger and more dapper than ever. He carried a cane which he swung back and forth in a rather affected way. In his buttonhole was a bright red carnation.

"Boy, did you ever see a more perfect getup,"

scoffed Annie.

There was one thing to spoil the general effect. Under his arm he carried a pair of shoes. He was certainly headed for the shoe shop. Uncle Jack stood next to the window watching the vision of fashion approach. As he reached the door, Uncle Jack gave an exclamation and turned deathly pale.

"What's the trouble, Uncle Jack? Are you sick?" Annie held his arm, trying to help him.

"I'm all right, Annie. Just let me sit down."

He hastened to the back of the shop and sat down on his work stool. Before Halk had got into the store, he had picked up a shoe and set to work on it. Annie wondered what could have happened to him. If he were sick he certainly wouldn't get to work, and yet he acted as though he had had a shock.

Mr. Halk was in a most genial mood. When he saw that Annie was there, he started teasing her about her mountain climbing. Evidently he had forgotten the idea that she was suspicious of him.

"I suppose you've done some exploring since I last saw you," he told her. "Or has your dog gone off alone to do his mountain climbing?"

"Neither of us has had any time for it," Annie said, trying not to show her dislike for him. "We've been busy helping Mr. Boot."

"Well, you remember when you do go exploring, you'd better stay clear of that old mine," Halk warned. "Everyone tells me it's close to falling down, and I know you youngsters would like to play in a spooky place like that. But it isn't safe for you. I think all the young ones should be warned to keep away from it."

He looked at Mr. Boot, evidently expecting him to agree. Annie looked around to see what Jack was thinking about this, and saw that he was working in such a position that his face was almost completely hidden.

Halk, too, noticed the queer position and stared hard at Jack. For a moment he seemed as puzzled as Annie, and then suddenly a gleam in his eye showed that he had discovered something. He fingered his mustache thoughtfully as he looked intently at Jack. He seemed vastly pleased with himself and finally he turned back to Annie, not having said a word to Jack.

"I want new lifts put on these heels," he told her, smiling his hard, glittery smile. "There's no hurry about it." He was facing Annie, but his words seemed meant for the shoemaker. "No hurry at all. I'll be around for a long time. Yes, a good long time."

Still stroking his mustache and gaily twirling his cane, he started for the door. With his hand on the knob he turned. "Good-by, Annie. Good-by, ah—," he hesitated as though he were trying to remember the name, and then with a sneer resumed, "Good-by, Mr. Boot."

"Good-by, Annie," Halk Said

"Oh, Uncle Jack, isn't he a horrid man?"

Annie ran to the side of the shoemaker. He still sat as he had on the arrival of Halk. On his forehead were beads of perspiration, and he seemed unable to speak. Annie still didn't know what it was all about, but she couldn't bear to see Uncle Jack like this, and she sobbed as she put her arms around him.

Seeing how frightened Annie had become, he pulled himself together.

"I'm all right, Annie. Don't cry. There's nothing to cry about. See, I'm all right."

He pulled her arms down from around his neck and stood up, still pale and shaken, but for Annie's sake making an effort to act natural.

"Come on, this has been enough for one day. Let's go home."

They locked the store and hand in hand the two set out for the little white house. Annie was still frightened by the effect Halk had had on Uncle Jack, and even more by that cold smile of Halk's when he had recognized the shoemaker. She wished she could tell Uncle Jack that she shared part of his secret. A hardship shared, she knew, was always easier to bear than one borne alone, but still she had no right to pry into affairs that were none of her business and she hated to admit what she had done.

At home the two got their supper. Annie chattered gaily to try to make Uncle Jack forget about his troubles, but though some of the color returned to his face, his eyes still had a faraway look to them. He ate next to nothing for his supper. When Annie scolded him and told him he'd be sick if he didn't eat, he looked at her blankly for a moment as though his mind had been far away from his kitchen. Finally he made a lame excuse about not being hungry. Annie saw that her visiting was doing no good, that Jack did not even hear her most of the time. She stopped trying to visit, and in silence they did the dishes together and tidied the kitchen.

Uncle Jack came out of his stupor long enough to say, "This has been a pretty big day for you, Annie. You'd better plan to go to bed early."

Seeing that Uncle Jack was finding an excuse to get rid of her, Annie agreed, and it was not long before she headed upstairs, trailed by Sandy.

Annie undressed and got into bed, but it was useless to try to sleep. She could hear Uncle Jack roaming around downstairs for a while; then everything was quiet. The quiet preyed on her nerves more than his roaming around had done. She worried that he might have become ill from worry, or harmed himself in some way. Finally she could stand the silence no longer. She slipped out of bed, and putting on a robe she crept carefully to the head of the stairs. Down below in the leather chair was Uncle Jack, one hand over his eyes, the other pounding on the arm of the

chair. Strewn about him on the floor were the book-
box and all the clippings. Annie heard him talking
to himself, and creeping down a few steps she heard
what sounded like a refain he had said over and over
again.

"What does he want of me? Why should he hound
me? He's been back of all this trouble. What can he
possibly do now?"

Annie crept back to her room as quietly as she
had left it. Sandy had followed her only as far as
the door and now he stood wagging his tail, waiting
for her.

She dropped down to the floor, and putting her
arms around him for comfort she cried, "If only I
could do something. If only he'd tell me about it so
I could help."

Finally, wiping her eyes she walked to the window
to look out at the stars. They always seemed to bring
her more comfort than anything else. Now as she
looked out she could see the light of the moon in
the garden, picking out a white blossom here and
there. Everything was at peace outside, except for
one thing. She looked again. Yes, at the back of the
yard was a spot of light that was not made by the
moon.

"Sandy, something's out in our back yard!" she
told the dog.

Sandy put his forefeet up on the window ledge

and looked out too. Soon his hair was bristling, and he growled a low growl deep in his throat.

"Who is it, Sandy? Can you tell?"

Annie wished more than ever that Sandy could talk. As she tried to decide what to do the light suddenly disappeared.

"Gee, I don't know now whether I should bother Uncle Jack or not. I guess I won't say anything unless the light comes again."

They waited for it to reappear, but there was nothing visible in the garden except the moonlight playing with the flowers.

"I guess maybe it wasn't anything, Sandy. No need to make him any more trouble. Let's go to bed."

Not feeling at all like sleeping she crept between the covers, but Sandy couldn't settle down. He paced back and forth in the room, looking out of the window occasionally. Annie had to tell him to lie down several times before he would obey her, and even then he twisted and turned as though there were not a comfortable place for him. Annie, too, was having difficulty getting to sleep. The more she thought, the worse she felt. Finally, though she told herself what a foolish thing it was, she was crying again, and eventually the sobbing must have put her to sleep.

When she awoke the next morning her eyes were still swollen from crying.

"But I'm not going to be such a baby again," she

told herself. "I'm not helping anyone that way. I've just got to remember that brave people are so busy setting wrong things right that they haven't time to cry about the wrong things."

She did remember it, too, for though her lip quivered when she thought of Uncle Jack's face the night before, she did no more crying. She hurried downstairs to see if Uncle Jack were all right, if he had been able to sleep at least part of the night.

She went through the front part of the house, but there was no Uncle Jack! She looked into the kitchen and then into his bedroom to see if he were still asleep. The bed had not been touched.

"Golly, something's happened! He's not here! Do you suppose that light did mean something last night?"

Anxiously she looked around for a clue. There was none. Everything looked exactly as it had the night before. The box had been returned to its shelf; nothing had been disturbed as far as she could see.

"I don't know what to do!" Annie moaned. "I don't even know where to start to look."

She searched the house again from top to bottom. She even peeked into the attic, which she had never seen before, but it was bare. She looked down cellar, but there was no sign of Uncle Jack. As she stepped back into the kitchen she thought of breakfast.

"I can't eat breakfast though, not knowing where

he is. I'm going to go down to the shoe store first. Maybe there will be a clue for me there."

With Sandy tight at her heels she started for the shop. She started out walking, but the farther she got the more worried she became and soon she was running as fast as her legs would carry her. When she reached the shop she stopped short and breathed a sigh of relief, for in the back of the shop a light was burning, and Uncle Jack was there hard at work on a pair of shoes.

She pushed the door open. "Uncle Jack!" she gasped. "You had me scared out of my wits."

Jack started as though he had not heard her come in. Then putting the shoe aside he smiled at her. It was a brave smile though back of it was pain and misery, but somehow Annie knew that he had come to some kind of agreement with himself and he felt better.

"Annie, you're down here early."

"Early, I should say so," sputtered Annie, thinking how worried she had been and of all the things she had thought might have happened to him. "I didn't know where you were or what had happened. Why didn't you tell me you were coming down here?"

"Annie, you know I never thought of frightening you," Jack apologized. "I couldn't sleep thinking about this pile of shoes you've got here for me, so I decided to come down and work."

Annie looked at the long line of shoes and knew that he had spent many hours of the night down here at his shop.

"You didn't even try to sleep," she couldn't help telling him. "Your bed hasn't been touched."

"I know. I was worried about something," he admitted, "and I can always figure better when my hands are busy. Don't worry, I'm all right."

Annie had to take that as a full account of the miserable night he must have spent, for he would tell her no more.

"Well, there's at least one thing I can do," Annie had become calm enough to do some thinking. "I can go home and get you some breakfast."

"I'm not hungry, Annie. Don't bother."

But Annie wouldn't listen to him. "Of course you're hungry! You didn't eat anything last night. You can't just starve yourself. Beside, I'm hungry," she added, discovering that she really was. "I'll bring down enough for two of us and we'll eat here in the shop."

It was a long time though before they got that breakfast, for just as Annie was starting out, the door was pushed open, and in walked Mr. Halk.

"Oh gosh, what now!" thought Annie.

In spite of his sudden entrance Jack was ready for him. He returned Halk's "Good morning" with a "Good morning, Mr. Halk," emphasizing the Mr. Halk in the same way Halk had emphasized "Mr.

Boot" the night before.

"I saw your light burning, and thought perhaps something was wrong. Thought perhaps I could help."

"Lots of help he's been!" thought Annie to herself.

"Oh no," Jack's voice was perfectly steady. He seemed as sure of himself as Halk now. "Just a little extra work to do. You're out pretty early yourself."

"Yes, I'm always up early. Early bird catches the worm you know. Nice time of day, early morning."

Annie could not help laughing herself. She knew this was serious business, but this over-politeness on both sides *was* funny when she knew they would rather be at each other's throats.

"Isn't he ever going?" she wondered. "I'm getting hungrier and hungrier, but I don't want to go until he does."

He seemed bent on staying. Annie thought it was queer that when there was such mutual dislike he should want to hang around the shop. As far as she could see there was nothing out of the ordinary about the conversation. It's true Halk did most of the talking, but there was nothing sinister or threatening about what he said. It was just ordinary talk about everyday happenings.

"This gets queerer and queerer," Annie reflected. "He must have something planned, coming here this way and visiting, but I just can't see any reason for it at all."

She considered going home anyway, but then she was afraid to leave the two alone. Finally she made up her mind to go. It was getting late. It had become light enough so that she could turn out the electric lights, and soon it would be time to open the store. She headed for the door. Halk, seeing her ready to go, looked at his watch, then smiled his cold glittery smile at her.

"Leaving already? Why I guess it is getting late. I'll be going too."

"How I hate that smile of his," thought Annie. "It's as though he knew something bad about you that you don't know yourself."

He went out of the store with her, and she dreaded having to visit with him, but after glancing down the way Annie had to go, he turned and went the opposite direction.

Annie suddenly discovered that she was all alone. Sandy had stayed with Uncle Jack. She was glad in a way, for she felt Uncle Jack needed protection from what she wasn't sure. There was something very, very queer about Mr. Halk, but she couldn't figure out what it was. Going up the street, she passed Halk's man, Ruff.

"There's something queer about him, too. He gives me the shivers, and he smiles just the way Halk does. They sure can't know anything about me though, and I can't see what good it would do them if they did know."

She ran up the steps of their little white house and pushed open the door. All she could do was gasp when she saw what lay before her. The floor was covered with books—all the lovely volumes from the shelves. Their pages had been ripped, and some had the leather torn from the back.

Annie was too stunned by the sight to know what to do. She walked dazedly over the books to the dining room and then on out into the kitchen. Everything was as she had left it. Jack's bedroom was all right, too. Nothing had been touched but the books. Suddenly it dawned on her—the box! Hurriedly she looked over the books on the floor. No box! She glanced up at the shelves. There were still a few books there. Dragging the leather chair over, she climbed up on it and lifted each book to feel its weight.

Yes, there it was! It hadn't been found. Sitting on an arm of the chair, her feet in the seat, she opened the box. It was empty! It had been found!

"I knew it!" cried Annie. "That's what Ruff was grinning about when he passed me. And that's why Halk was so anxious to talk to us at the store. He wanted to be sure to give Ruff enough time."

All the pieces fitted into place now. They always do when it's too late. Annie could guess too why that light had appeared in the back yard.

"I should have told Uncle Jack. They must have stood right under the window watching him. No wonder there's nothing touched but the books. They knew just what to look for."

Angry and disgusted at the way those two had put something over on them she headed back to the store to tell Uncle Jack.

"How that Halk could pull the wool over our eyes that way I can't see," she mourned. "When he looked at his watch just as I was going out I should have guessed something was up. Now I know he knows about Uncle Jack's past, but I can't see what good it will do him now. It isn't as though Uncle Jack hadn't served his sentence, or hadn't been caught."

She paused to consider what she had been saying to herself. It almost sounded as if she were admitting that Uncle Jack had been guilty.

"But I know that's not true. I know Uncle Jack wouldn't do a thing like that. And if Halk is going to try to bother him, I'm going to stop him. I don't know how, but I'll try my best!"

Her entrance to the store was as flustered and hurried as it had been earlier in the morning.

"Uncle Jack," she cried, her words tumbling over each other, "that Ruff's been in our house."

Uncle Jack couldn't understand what she was talking about at first.

She Hurried into the Store

"Now, now, Annie, calm down. Start at the beginning and tell me."

Annie was too excited and too angry to tell a calm story.

"That's why that old Halk was so friendly. No wonder he stayed here so long."

"Annie, Annie, you aren't making sense. What happened?"

Annie, seeing that she still hadn't made him realize what had happened, started at the beginning.

"On my way home for breakfast I met Ruff coming this way."

"Yes, Halk walked along slowly until Ruff caught up to him. I watched him," Jack confessed.

"Well, when I got to the house, I opened the door and there everything was."

Jack began to see what she was trying to tell him. He turned pale but his voice was still calm as he asked, "What did they look at, Annie?"

"Every book in the place, I think. They're almost all on the floor, and some of them are all torn and ripped.

She didn't dare tell him that the important one had been found. She still couldn't tell him that she too knew the secret of his books.

Jack said not a word for a minute. Then finally he laughed a shaky laugh and as though he were talking to himself said, "So he had to have proof, did he?"

"I'm going to call the sheriff." Annie started, but Jack stopped her.

"No, no, Annie. I think I know what's missing. It won't do any good to call him."

"But, Uncle Jack, it's a robbery, isn't it? The sheriff ought to know about it." Her pleading did no good. Jack would not hear of letting anyone know about it.

"I'll go home and see what's missing. I think I know what I'll find. It's nothing important."

Leaving Annie to take care of the store, he left.

"How he can be so calm about it I can't see. Of course he knows what's missing, and he says it isn't important. Why, I think that's just about the most important thing in his life. I can see why he wouldn't want the town to know. If they knew he was James Burn they'd drive him out in a hurry. It's funny he would come back here anyway after everything that happened."

There were certainly mysteries in Uncle Jack's life about which she knew nothing. There was only one thing of which she was sure. Uncle Jack would never willingly do something wrong. Halk and Ruff were a different story. Annie was sure they would do anything that meant money for them. She thought of all the things she would like to do to those two. She was sure that anything she could think of would be too good for them.

"Now that they've got that box I suppose we can

expect something else to happen. If Uncle Jack knows what they're up to, I wish he'd tell me. This feeling that something's going to strike, but not knowing what, is like sitting on the edge of a volcano."

A few customers came and went. Annie's body waited on them and her voice answered them, but she was so busy thinking that she hardly noticed they were there. She said, "Yes, it's going to be a nice day," and "Your shoes will be ready Monday," but her brain was saying, "Why do they want the box? What can they do to Uncle Jack?"

She was not very busy. Few customers are around early in the morning. Besides, many of the people who might have come had been taken care of by Annie's new delivery service. About ten-thirty Mrs. Speedle came down the street. Annie saw her coming. She had no shoes with her, and Annie knew she already had the pair that she had brought in the first day she had been at the store. As usual she came in all a-twitter. Annie thought at first that somehow she had found out about the robbery, and was coming to get more information, but that was one thing she hadn't found out about. She was on quite a different errand.

"I came down to take another look at you, Annie," Mrs. Speedle began.

"Oh, oh, here it comes," thought Annie. "It never rains put it pours. She's found out I'm not related to

Uncle Jack."

She was mistaken about that, too. So many bad things had happened that she expected everything to be bad. This was entirely different.

"Annie, I've got a big favor to ask of you," Mrs. Speedle gushed, more as though she were bestowing a favor than asking one. "Little Janet Bolker caught the measles somewhere and she was going to serve at the tea tomorrow."

Annie had forgotten about the literary tea for Mr. Halk. Neither she nor Uncle Jack had been invited so the occasion hadn't made much of an impression on her.

"I hate to ask you this at the last minute, but I thought you were just about Janet's size, and we got dresses especially made for it. We thought maybe you'd like to take Janet's place."

"Huh," thought Annie, "thanks for wanting me for my own sweet self." But aloud she said, "Why, of course, I'll help you out." She could bestow favors too when she wanted to. "I'm not doing anything special tomorrow afternoon. I'll be glad to help you out, Mrs. Speedle."

"Well, then." Now that she had what she had come for Mrs. Speedle was in a hurry to leave. "You come over the first thing tomorrow morning so that I can show you just how to serve things. We don't want any slip-ups tomorrow afternoon. Everything must be done just right."

"I'll come as early as I can." Annie was none too enthusiastic.

As she went out Annie thought she overheard something about a pink dress.

"Horrors!" exclaimed Annie. "Pink dress and my red hair. Everything must be just right! It's going to be just beautiful!"

The more she thought about the invitation the more she resented it. "She sounds as though I didn't know anything about politeness or etiquette."

In her indignation Annie almost forgot the early morning happenings. It wasn't like Annie to let little people like Mrs. Speedle upset her. She scolded herself because after all where would Mrs. Speedle get a chance to find out about high society, and how could she know that Annie would naturally know how to act? Most children Annie's age would be petrified to think of doing anything like this.

"Besides, I didn't have to do it. I offered to quick enough. I brought it on myself." Just then she had a happy thought. "And anyway, Mr. Halk's got to be there since he's the guest of honor, and if I want to keep my eye on him, what better place is there?"

By the time Jack came back, Annie had calmed down considerably. Jack, too, seemed calm though his eyes still held that worried look that Annie hated to see.

"Was anything else—" Annie broke off realizing she was making a blunder. Then she hurriedly turned her sentence around. "Was anything else upset beside the books?"

"No, but they certainly made a mess of them, didn't they? I put them back on the shelves, except for the ripped ones that I'll have to fix. I'll mend them as soon as I have a little more time."

"Did they take anything?" Annie had her question worded carefully this time.

"Well, I guess they got what they came for, but it isn't important, and much good it can do them!"

"I don't know how he can be so calm about it," thought Annie. "Those men have his whole past record and they can make things very miserable for him."

"Only a book, nothing important."

"But even so shouldn't we call the sheriff?" Annie knew what the answer would be before she asked the question. "Even if it was only a book they took, they wrecked your house. They shouldn't get away with that."

"What proof have we who did it? Just because Halk made us an early morning call is no proof that his man was busy going through our house. No, don't you say anything about it. If you even suggested that Halk had anything to do with it you'd find the village on your neck. Look what happened to poor Miss Jens when she suggested he hadn't written a book. No one in the village will have anything to do with her."

"Oh gee, with all this excitement I forgot to tell you—I've got a job for tomorrow."

"A job! What kind of a job? It's Sunday."

"I know it, but I'm going to the *tea*."

"The tea!" Jack looked at her in astonishment and Annie laughed at his expression.

"You didn't know I'd made a hit around town, too, did you?" Annie teased, and then not feeling much like playing, she told him of the special invitation she had received.

Jack thought the whole affair was a good joke, and Annie, who had been raging inside about it, began to see the funny side of it too. Soon they were both laughing over it and when Annie came to the *pink dress* she had to collapse on a bench, weak with giggling.

Jack was the first to recover.

"You know, I'm glad you're going to have something to do tomorrow, because I'm going to be gone all day."

"Gone? Where?"

"I thought I'd go up in the hills. Maybe do some hunting."

"Hunting! I didn't know you hunted. What are you going to hunt?"

"Oh, anything that happens along. Thought it

would be a change from the village," and Jack returned to the subject of the tea without telling any more about his plans.

CHAPTER FIVE

THE TEA PARTY

Annie was up bright and early next morning. She had told herself the night before she was going to get up before Uncle Jack did, so that she could get him a good breakfast and pack a lunch for him. She did beat him, too. The coffee was all made before he appeared at the kitchen door dressed in his oldest clothes.

"That coffee certainly smells good, Annie," he told her. Annie felt well repaid for her early rising.

"Where's your gun?" Annie wanted to know as they sat down to breakfast.

"I'm not taking a gun. I guess you'd call this expedition a trapping expedition rather than a hunting one."

"I still would like to know what you're going to hunt or trap or whatever," Annie told him.

"Well," Uncle Jack smiled. "Do you know what a gila monster is?"

"Oh sure, it's some kind of a lizard—poisonous, isn't it?"

"That's right. And that's what I'm hunting for."

"Go on, they're all out West. There aren't any in

100

the East."

"Ha, ha, you know your nature study pretty well, don't you? Nevertheless, whether you believe me or not, that's what I'm planning to trap—a gila monster."

"All right, if you say so," Annie told him," but I still don't believe you."

Uncle Jack couldn't help teasing, "If I do catch him, I'll lead him down here on the end of a rope. Then you'll have to believe me."

"Well, seeing's believing, I guess, but I'm pretty sure I won't see him."

"I certainly hope you *do*." Jack's voice was no longer teasing; it was deadly serious.

"Shall I take Sandy with me?" he wanted to know as he got ready to leave.

"Oh, he'd love it," Annie told him. "And I'd just have to shut him up in the house. I couldn't let him follow me over to Mrs. Speedle's. She doesn't like him. Sure, take him."

Calling to Sandy, Jack started out. Annie noticed that he had a coiled length of rope fastened to his belt.

"To bring the gila monster back?" she asked him, but actually she wondered if that meant he was heading for the mine.

She hurried to get the house straightened, for she was due at Mrs. Speedle's for instructions.

"No use getting her sore at me for coming late," she thought, but she thought more about Jack's trip than she did about the tea. The word "gila monster" danced around in her head, but she could find no hidden meaning for it. Yet Uncle Jack had turned deadly serious while he was talking about it.

"Oh well, I'll find out about it sometime," Annie decided.

As soon as she could she started for Mrs. Speedle's. She was not the first one there. Mrs. Bolker and Mary Lou Bart were already there.

"It would have to be Mary Lou!" thought Annie.

Mary Lou was the only child of the town's bank president. She had everything she wanted, which was considerable, and her attitude was that she was far better than anyone else in town. That wasn't entirely her fault, for her mother, who was the town's social leader, told everyone what a child wonder Mary Lou was.

"O'course, she had to be in on this," thought Annie. "Mrs. Speedle would have to have her or Mrs. Bart wouldn't come to the party or wouldn't invite her to any other parties."

Mrs. Bart was already put out because Mrs. Speedle had thought of the party before she had. Evidently having Mary Lou serve was the price paid for appeasing her.

Annie liked her job less and less. Mrs. Speedle was busy frosting a big chocolate cake.

"You stay over there by the door until I'm ready

for you, Annie. Don't get in my way."

Mary Lou was seated on a high stool near the table. She didn't bother to say hello to Annie. Mrs. Bolker was cutting sandwiches into tiny diamonds.

"Oh, I'm so angry at Janet," she mourned. "Why did she have to get measles now of all times. You should see her face—it's just covered today."

"And she and Mary Lou would have made such a darling pair," Mrs. Speedle commented. "Mary Lou is so fair, and Janet's hair is so dark. They would have looked adorable together."

"Well, we'll just have to get along as best we can." Mrs. Bolker looked at Annie's red mop with distaste. "Let's hope the dress fits, at least."

"All right, let's leave this and go try it. I guess I'd feel better if I knew the worst right away. Come on, Annie. Let's see what you look like in it."

Mary Lou climbed off her seat and came too. Her dress was pale blue and would be nice with her fair hair. Annie shook her head when she saw her dress. It was a mass of organdy ruffles from the waist down— *pink* organdy ruffles. Janet would have looked like a fairy in it, but Annie knew what it would do to her.

"Gee, Mrs. Speedle, are you sure you want me to wear that?" Annie looked at the dress ruefully.

"Of course, we want you to wear it. If it hadn't been for the dress you wouldn't have had to help at all." Mrs. Speedle was anything but tactful. "Mary

Lou has her blue one. We bought the pink one especially to go with it. Here, try it on, Annie. Careful—don't muss the ruffles."

With Mrs. Speedle's help Annie got the dress on. It did fit. Mrs. Speedle had been pretty accurate in guessing Annie's size. And it was a dream of a dress. It was the kind of dress every little girl dreams of, but it was not the kind Annie was meant to wear.

"Why, it doesn't look so bad," said Mrs. Bolker, and Annie silently thanked her for that much, but Mrs. Speedle couldn't be that generous. Janet's treachery in having measles had certainly spoiled her party for her.

"Well, it will have to do. There's nothing else we can do about it. Take it off, Annie, so you won't get it dirty before it's time for the party."

She headed back to the kitchen to finish frosting her cake. Mrs. Bolker helped Annie take the dress off and carefully hung it in the closet. When Annie finished dressing she returned to the kitchen. The women were hard at work. Mrs. Speedle had finished frosting her cake. Mary Lou was perched on her high stool, and in her lap was the frosting bowl. As Annie came out she lifted a big spoonful of thick frosting to her mouth and grinned at Annie. No one suggested that Annie help clean out the bowl. She stood against the wall as far out of the way as she could get, and watched Mary Lou lick and scrape to her heart's

Annie Tried on the Ruffled Dress

content.

"I wish I were up the mountain with Uncle Jack," thought Annie. "I certainly wasn't cut out to be a social butterfly, I guess. I hate this."

The long morning wore away. The two girls were taken to the parlor to practice. They handed the plate with a cup filled with water (for practice) on it to Mrs. Bolker, who played guest a countless number of times. Annie did all the motions with an ease and grace that astonished the two women. Mrs. Speedle found fault though. She couldn't forgive Annie for not being Janet Bolker. She picked at this and that while Mary Lou stood by and smiled sweetly. It seemed that every time Mrs. Speedle looked at the red hair she grew more displeased, and Annie could feel the temper that went with that red hair rising.

"I just have to take it though," she cautioned herself. "I was the one who offered to do it and I knew what I was getting into."

Patiently she let Mrs. Speedle correct her and scold her while she praised Mary Lou and wished for Janet.

At last they ate lunch, the tails from the sandwiches and little else. Then it was time to dress.

"Another two hours and it will be over," thought Annie, "and boy, will I be glad."

She stood quietly while Mrs. Bolker slipped the pink ruffles over her head, and combed her hair into as much order as she could. It was not a sleek head of hair like Mary Lou's. The curls refused to stay down. They bobbed up all over her head as fast as Mrs. Bolker combed them down.

Mary Lou sat primly waiting for the guests to come, but Annie was not so comfortable. She stood at the window, careful not to muss the ruffles against the sill. She wasn't used to just sitting with nothing to do.

"I wish they'd hurry up and come," she told Mary Lou.

Mary Lou had said no more than a dozen words to her all morning, but evidently the waiting was bothering her too and she decided to spend the time impressing Annie.

"Mama said I could recite for Mr. Halk after we're done serving. Mamma says I should be an actress or maybe she'll take me out to Hollywood and get me a part in the movies."

Annie knew all about Hollywood and its "mama's darlings."

"I'll bet she'd make a good one all right. She could drive the directors stark raving mad," thought Annie, "and I'll bet she does say her piece this afternoon, too. Since Mrs. Bart's her mother there's nothing much Mrs. Speedle or Mrs. Bolker dare do about it."

The girls were shooed out of the parlor before anyone arrived. The curtains between the two rooms were closed. Annie found that the dining-room window gave her a view of the walk. As the guests started arriving the girls found they could easily hear the conversation going on in the front room too. Mary Lou left without a grown-up to watch her no longer sat quietly on a chair. She opened the curtains far enough to see into the living-room and report to Annie what everyone was wearing. When her mother arrived Mary Lou let out a loud "Pssst" which undoubtedly everyone in the parlor heard, and her mother came over to the door to give her a fond kiss.

At last everyone had arrived except the guest of honor. There would be a great deal of talking and then someone would mention Mr. Halk's name and everyone paused to see if he were coming. Finally the big car drove up outside the house.

"Only two blocks to walk and he brings the car to impress us," thought Annie.

Mr. Halk didn't get out right away. He leaned over the front seat and talked to Ruff. They seemed to be arguing about something.

"There's one thing to spoil that picture of success," Annie decided. "A real chauffeur wouldn't act that way."

Finally after a good deal of talking Ruff nodded in reluctant agreement and Halk got out. With a great grinding of gears and an unnecessary burst of speed Ruff left Halk standing on the curb.

Halk was dressed with even more care than usual.

Over his arm he carried his cane; he had a fresh red carnation in his buttonhole; his striped trousers, his gray felt hat, his gloves, everything was the height of perfection, and among the waiting ladies there were "oh's" and "ah's" of admiration.

"A whole half hour late!" Annie liked him less and less. "A whole half hour late so that he can make a grand entrance."

And a grand entrance it was. The women gathered around him, each trying to claim his attention. He seemed to like it, too, and this pushed him even lower in Annie's estimation. Finally he was relieved of his hat and cane and gloves, and he sat down in the big overstuffed chair that had been saved for the guest of honor.

"He's the only man here," marveled Annie.

"Of course, silly," Mary Lou told her. "Most men are so silly. My daddy said he'd be seen dead before he'd come to a tea with a lot of giggling women."

"I wonder where all the men are this afternoon," said Annie, thinking that she would rather be with them than where she was.

"Oh, they're most of them down at the sheriff's office playing cards. They said they might as well have a party of their own since the women were having one.

"But be quiet, can't you," the spoiled little girl said. "I want to listen to what they're talking about."

They didn't have much chance to listen, for Mrs. Speedle came out to start them serving.

"And don't forget how to do it, Annie," Mrs. Speedle whispered just as Annie was going through the door to the living-room.

As she went in and out with the plates, Annie heard bits of the conversation. Over in Halk's corner he had turned the talk around to the old mine again. Annie wished she could stay to listen, but she didn't dare, for Mrs. Speedle kept an eye on her constantly.

Just as Annie was coming in, a plate with a steaming cupful of tea on it in each hand, she overheard a fragment of conversation that made her stop dead in her tracks. One of the women had just mentioned Horace Gila, Uncle Jack's partner at the mine. All of a sudden the whole thing cleared up for Annie—a gila monster—Horace Gila—that's what Uncle Jack was trapping.

Annie was so surprised that she stopped right in the middle of the floor. She thought she saw Halk start, too, but things happened so fast that afterward she couldn't be sure. Mary Lou had been right behind her with two more plates, but she had been so busy looking at Mr. Halk that she hadn't seen Annie stop. She bumped square into Annie, the hot tea going all down the front of the ruffly blue dress. She let out a scream and her mother and Mrs. Speedle went to her at once.

"Poor dear," said Mrs. Speedle, sending Annie for a cloth to wipe up the mess and trying to comfort the sobbing Mary Lou. "That clumsy girl! I knew we'd have trouble."

The ladies made a great fuss over Mary Lou. Annie apologized as best she could, but everyone blamed her entirely. It made no difference that Mary Lou had paid no attention to where she was going.

Mary Lou had not been burned; for that Annie was thankful. But the blue ruffles had turned a dirty brown, and they no longer stood out in neat rows. The only thing that was hurt was Mary Lou's vanity. Her sobbing was more from rage about the spoiled dress than from pain. Finally the women succeeded in drying her clothes and her tears, and she was settled in the seat of honor, the footstool at Mr. Halk's feet, where undoubtedly she spent the rest of the afternoon. Mrs. Speedle and Mrs. Bolker finished bringing in the plates themselves, for Mary Lou (poor dear) was too upset to be trusted, and certainly they couldn't trust Annie again. Why, the next thing they knew she might pour something down a guest's neck.

When they had finished serving, Mrs. Speedle took time out to banish Annie to the kitchen.

"I'm not going to have you disgrace us any more. What must Mr. Halk think of us! I'd just like to know if you did that on purpose!"

Annie, left alone in the kitchen, didn't know what to do.

"I guess the best thing for me to do is to get out of here," she decided.

She found her own dress hanging in the bedroom, and carefully taking the ruffly dress off she hung it on a hanger and slipped into her own.

"I don't know when I've been so ashamed of myself," she thought. "How will I ever tell Uncle Jack about it?"

She went out the back door and walked dejectedly toward home, one foot dragging behind the other. She knew what it would be like to face the townspeople after today's blunder.

"But that did startle me so," Annie inwardly excused herself. "After I'd thought so hard about the gila monster, and couldn't make anything out of it, and then when I'd forgotten all about it to have it pop just like that—I couldn't help being surprised."

Dreading to go home she walked down through town, steering clear of the sheriff's office where all the men had assembled. She passed Uncle Jack's shop and the railway station; she went on out toward the hills and climbed slowly to the place where she had first seen the town. There she stood, a desolate little figure, not even Sandy to comfort her, looking down at Butternut. As on the first night, she saw the lights start to go on down in the valley, but somehow they did not look as friendly as they had that first night. Each one seemed to be accusing her. Above all the rest the one that Annie picked out as coming from Mrs. Speedle's house shone with an especially baleful eye.

Annie's mind was awhirl with all the things that had happened during the day, but gradually the quiet of the coming night descending over the valley, descended on her as well, and finding a rock for a seat she turned her thoughts back to the day she had come to Butternut. It had been less than a week ago, but it seemed as though she had been part of Butternut for a long time.

Gradually as she looked at the valley, in the back of her mind she seemed to sense that something was wrong with this picture she was seeing tonight.

"It isn't the way it was when I was up here before," she pondered, "but I can't figure out what's different. It's as though I'd seen a picture and then when it was shown to me again something had been cut out."

Suddenly she realized what it was. The first night she had seen this picture the train had come through, a long snake shining in the dark. She had heard its whistle and seen it pulling into the station. Tonight she had heard nothing of it. She had learned that Butternut had just two trains a day—one in the morning going north (that was the one she had heard just before she had found the mine), the other at this time of night.

"It's probably late," guessed Annie, though in the time she had been in Butternut it had always been right on schedule. "I'll wait until it goes through and then I'll go home."

She sat there quietly. The dark was creeping slowly up the mountainside. There was a calmness about this time of night that felt as though everything were holding its breath, waiting for something to happen. Annie too almost held her breath waiting to hear the first far-off whistle of the train.

"Something must have happened to it," she decided. "It must be a half hour late by this time. I suppose I ought to go home."

Somehow, though, when you set out to wait for something, you feel you've got to wait until it happens. Annie gave herself ten more minutes, and when she thought those were up, gave herself another five. She'd tell herself she must start for home, for the stony road was not too inviting to travel at night, but she had to stay a few minutes more.

Finally she knew she could sit there no longer. Slowly she started down the road, hoping that the train would go through while she was still high enough to watch it curl around the bend down into the valley. She had almost reached the first houses of the town, though, when far in the distance she heard its mournful whistle. She stopped to listen to it. Usually it whistled just once to warn the town it was approaching, and once when it got near the mountain road crossing, but tonight as Annie listened, it kept up its whistling, one toot after another.

Annie wasn't the only one who heard the sound. Evidently both the tea and the men's card game had been over for some time, for from the lighted houses along the street men and children rushed out, listened to the tooting and then headed toward the station. The women stood on the porches, calling to each other, and a few of them decided to go with the men. Annie started to run, but before she reached the station half the town had beat her, and the train—or rather part of the train—was thundering to a stop at the platform.

CHAPTER SIX

THE ROBBERY

Annie found herself back at the edge of the crowd. She could see little of what was going on up in front. She could tell that there was just part of the train there—the engine and the express car.

"Gee, that's funny," she thought. "Maybe they had a wreck and this engine part came in for help."

But no one seemed to be getting doctors or stretchers ready. The men would swing down from the train, their lighted lanterns in their hands, but she could not hear what was being said up near the track. The people around her had found out as little as she had.

"If I could find a place where I could see over people's heads," she thought.

She edged around the crowd to the station. She could see nothing more from here, but finally she discovered the window of the express room that looked out over the tracks. If she could climb up there she'd be able to sit on the ledge and see over other people's heads.

Lifting her skirts out of the way she pulled herself part way up to the window ledge. Hanging there try-

ing to boost herself the rest of the way up she glanced
in the lighted window. There was no movement in
there, but to her horror she saw something stretched
out on the floor.

"Gee, that's the station agent!" she cried, but everyone was so excited they didn't hear her. She let go
of the window ledge and dropped back to the ground
with a thud.

"Hey," she tried to get the attention of the people
around her. "The station agent—"

She pulled at men's coats but they paid no attention, probably thinking she wanted to ask them what
was happening.

"Golly, you've got to listen!" sobbed Annie.

Just then one of the trainmen with his lantern
pushed his way through the crowd toward the station.

"What's up?"

"What happened?"

"Is there a wreck?"

Everyone grabbed at him, but he brushed them
off, too busy to worry about them. As he pushed past
Annie she grabbed his arm with all her strength.

"Look out, kid, I'm busy!" He tried to pull away
from her, but she held tight. Angrily he yanked away
from her and with a stinging hand she let go.

"The express office," she yelled at him, sticking
tight to his heels.

She need not have bothered, for that's where he

was heading anyway. Annie followed close behind him, taking advantage of the pathway he made for her. As he got near the express room window Annie yelled, "Look in the window."

Almost without realizing he was obeying her he looked.

"Charley!" he gasped and raced for the door. He bent over the still figure on the floor, and then in a voice that could be heard over the din outside he yelled, "Hey, Bill—Tony."

The two he had called elbowed their way through the crowd. Seeing that there was more going on inside the station than outside, the people pushed toward the office door. Annie had followed the first man into the room and stood crowded against the wall next to the door. One of the men, Bill or Tony, saw the crowd heading for the doorway and put his big body square in the middle of it, with an arm stretched out to the door frame on each side.

"Oh, no, you don't," he told them as some of the people in front tried to get past him to see what was inside.

The man Annie had grabbed was at the telephone. "Bob Harding—number six," he reported. "We were held up—three miles north of Butternut. Yep, got the gold shipment."

Though you could still hear the buzz of talk from outside, the people near the door had discovered

"Look at the Window!" Annie Yelled

that the telephone was carrying the news, and they almost held their breath to see what was being reported.

"Got the safe combination from the agent—he's out cold. Haven't checked yet, the sheriff will be here in a minute. Sure, right at the turn before the mountain road. Five fellows. All wore masks. They'd hauled a log across the tracks. Yah, shot the messenger. There was a doctor on the train; we left him there. Yah, I'll report back. Hold the line open."

Those near the door of the office heard what he had reported. You could hear the news going back through the crowd and the excited buzzing on the platform rose to a higher pitch.

Annie heard, "That's where the other robbery was."

"Gold shipment that time too."

Then she heard what she had been fearing might follow as she had listened to the report.

"Sounds as though James Burn was back again."

Mrs. Speedle had been right when she said people thought Burn had done the robbery too.

"Poor Uncle Jack," thought Annie. "This is going to be bad for him. I've got to tell him before he hears it from someone else."

She ducked her head to get under the arm of the man at the door, but the movement caught the eye of the man she had grabbed.

"Hey, hold her!" he yelled, and the big fellow at the door put down one hand and the strength of it warned Annie that she had better stand still.

She turned to face the man who had ordered her stopped.

"What do you know about this?" he demanded.

"Nothing, I just looked in and saw him."

Annie shuddered as she looked at the still form on the floor.

The trainman eyed the height of the window and then Annie. Seeing he was wondering how she had looked through the window, she told him how it had happened. He asked question after question.

"Had she been there before the rest?" "Was there anyone else in the room?" "Had she seen anyone come out?"

She could truthfully answer no to all his questions, but she could hear the people behind her whispering and doubting. Once she had been afraid of rousing gossip in the village. Now she had certainly succeeded in doing just that. She had been so glad that no one had noticed or wondered about her, and now here she was drawing attention to herself the second time in one day. And it was anything but favorable attention, too.

Finally the man made up his mind that she knew nothing more and let her go. She wedged her way out through the crowd. She could feel the cold unfriendly stares and hear the sly whispers as she went past the people, especially those who had attended the tea. Everyone was ready to believe the worst about her, and just being in the office and questioned was enough to assure them that she had something to do with the holdup.

She searched through the crowd for Uncle Jack, thinking that with all the excitement he would probably have come down too, but she couldn't find him. Neither could she see a sign of Ruff or Halk. She did see her pal Mary Lou at the edge of the platform, where she was trying to crawl up to the door of the express car.

"Have you seen Uncle Jack, Mary Lou?" Annie called.

Mary Lou turned around, saw who it was, and gave her a cold stare.

"What's it to you?" was all the answer Annie got.

Annie tried other groups. Each person gave her a queer look as she asked her question, but they answered her. No one had seen Uncle Jack, and neither had they seen Mr. Halk. Finally giving up, she started toward home. Evidently both Uncle Jack and Halk had stayed away from the excitement.

"I've got to warn Uncle Jack," thought Annie. "If someone mentioned Burn and this robbery he'd give himself away sure. If only Halk would stay away we'd be pretty safe, but with him knowing, no telling what may happen."

All of a sudden something seemed very clear to her.

"That's why Halk was so anxious to get proof. Halk was mixed up in this and he was going to put the blame on Uncle Jack alias James Burn."

Too frightened to cry she raced for the house. Past the shoe shop, past the old Burn house she sped. She headed diagonally across the street for home and had to jump back to the curb as a car came racing down from the mountain road. As it tore past her she saw it was Halk's car and she caught a glimpse of his gray hat and red carnation as it whirled past.

"He wasn't around the station then!" she decided. "He was up in the mountains some place."

She hastened on to warn Jack, but when she turned in at the path she discovered that the house was dark. There was not a sign of Uncle Jack or Sandy.

"Golly, I've got to tell him," she thought as she searched through the house hoping to find that he had been home. "He's got to know about it before the villagers start getting suspicious."

There seemed no chance to tell him, for though she waited and worried for over an hour no one appeared. She could picture all the things that might have happened to him; he could have fallen down into the mine, or he might have met Halk and got into a fight—any number of the things could have happened. Each thought was worse than the one before. Every once in a while she'd go to the door to see if she could see him, but the night was so dark that if he had been coming she couldn't have seen him until he reached the path. As she stood at the doorway looking toward the hills, she saw a dark shape come pell mell through the yard.

"That's Sandy!" she recognized the shape, but there was no Uncle Jack behind him. His coat was dirty and bedraggled as though he had crawled through underbrush. From his right ear trickled a little stream of blood.

"Oh, Sandy, what's happened?" cried Annie, bending down to look at the wound. She gave an exclamation as she discovered that it was no ordinary tear; it was a bullet hole!

"Sandy, what's happened? Where's Uncle Jack?"

But of course Sandy couldn't answer. He crept out to the kitchen, found his pan of water and lay down under the stove. Annie washed his wound and sterilized it. As she worked she tried to decide what had happened and what she ought to do.

"Maybe they've hurt Uncle Jack," she thought, not questioning that "they" was anyone but Halk and Ruff. "I've got to get to him."

She put on a warm jacket and hunted for an old lantern she had seen down in the cellar. Sandy got up stiffly and followed her out the door.

"Go on back, Sandy. You stay home," said Annie.

He was lame and tired and worn out, but he would not be sent home. If Annie were going into danger he had to follow her.

The mountain road was harder than ever to climb at night. Annie couldn't see the stones that found their way to the surface of the road, and she had stubbed her toe many times and tripped over a tree root in the road before she reached the spot from which she had viewed the village a few hours earlier. She sat down on the big rock to rest for a moment and Sandy flopped beside her. Looking down the tracks she could see two lanterns close to the bend of the road. Evidently they were two searchers looking for the path the bandits had taken after leaving the train. She pulled herself to her feet and started on. She wound her way up between the rocks that towered higher and higher on each side of her. Exhausted she would sit down to rest, but her worry for Uncle Jack forced her to her feet and she would start again, giving Sandy, who had traveled this trail before today, little chance to get his breath.

They were both panting hard when against the dark sky she caught sight of the dim outline of the shaft house. There was no sound or light that she could see. Cautiously she moved toward it. She had been afraid to light her lantern for fear someone might see her, and now she was glad that she hadn't, for as the ground leveled out she thought she saw a figure crouched in the scrub pine near the road. It was almost the same spot where she and Sandy had hidden from Halk and Ruff when they had first been at the mine. Yes, it was a figure. Annie saw it move. She crouched at the edge of the road, hoping she had been mistaken, but suddenly she heard a low "Pssst."

She held her breath, wondering what would happen next. The sound came again.

"Pssst."

The figure back in the bushes was moving toward her. Then she heard a low tone, "Annie."

It was Uncle Jack's voice! Happy with relief Annie started toward him.

"Get down!" Though his voice was low it carried the sound of command. "Hurry, but keep low," he instructed.

Working her way through the stunted pines she reached him. He had picked the exact spot that she had used the other day.

"What are you doing here?" He was anything but glad to see her. Not giving her time to answer he asked, "Did you see those fellows on the road?"

"What fellows? I didn't see anybody."

"But you must have. There's no turn off from the road."

Annie shook her head. "Who were they?" she whispered.

Uncle Jack covered her mouth with his hand. She

turned to see why and saw two figures silhouetted against the road. She thought she recognized the stride of Ruff, but she wasn't sure. The other one certainly wasn't Halk, and Annie didn't think he looked at all familiar. Sandy too had seen them and recognized his old enemy Ruff. Annie had not held on to him; in fact, she had been so busy with Uncle Jack that she had forgotten about him. Suddenly, as tired as he was, snarling he leaped at Ruff. Taken by surprise, Ruff stepped back, but in a second his hand went to his hip and he drew his revolver. Annie started to scream to warn Sandy who was trying to reach Ruff, but again Jack's hand was clapped over her mouth.

"Don't be a fool, Annie. You can't help. You'll get us killed too."

The gun did not go off, for as Ruff tried to aim at the leaping dog the stranger with him grabbed his arm.

"What are you trying to do? Bring the whole neighborhood up here? You got told once before not to do that again. Now let's have that gun."

"Who do you think you're ordering around?" Ruff retorted, his voice cold with anger. "Since when are you bossing this outfit?"

"No, I'm not bossing the outfit and neither are you, but you know right well who is, and he told you no more shooting. If you know what's good for you, you'll give me that gun so you won't be tempted again."

Ruff was certainly having troubles, with Sandy before him, snarlingly waiting for an opening, and this companion at his side trying to get his gun. Evidently being reminded of the boss bore some weight, for Ruff slipped the gun back into his pocket, ignoring the other's outstretched hand waiting for it. Furiously he kicked at Sandy, who was still lunging at him unsuccessfully. It was a lucky kick, for it landed, and with a tired sigh Sandy dropped back and fell at the edge of the road.

"That dog's been snooping around all day. There's something funny about him. I don't like him."

"It doesn't look as though he'd trouble you for a while. Come on, let's get inside, but for Pete's sake keep that gun in your pocket."

Annie would have gone to Sandy at once, but Jack held her back. The men walked on up the road and Ruff turned around once to see if Sandy were still there. Evidently he still didn't feel too safe with the dog around. Annie was glad she hadn't quit their hiding place. The two headed straight for the doorway of the shaft house. Annie thought she saw a third man join them just at the door.

"Is that another one?" she wanted to know.

"There are two besides," Jack whispered, keeping his eyes on the figures.

Finally all of them went in.

"Now's your chance. Take a look at Sandy and then get down that mountain as fast as you can."

"Shall I bring the sheriff?"

"Don't you say a word. You get down there and if I'm not back tomorrow you open the store. I'll be down just as soon as I find out what I want to know."

Annie crept to Sandy, who was trying to get to his feet. Evidently the wind had been knocked out of him, but no bones seemed to be broken, for though he was wobbly he managed to walk.

She went back to report to Uncle Jack, but he was angry with her for returning. "If he's O.K. take him along but hurry up and get out of here."

"What about you? Will you be all right?"

"I'll be all right. Just do what I ask and hurry!" There was nothing much for her to do but follow directions. She went down the mountain road as fast as she dared. Sandy dragged behind her and she slowed so that he could keep up. She didn't dare stop, though, with the orders Jack had given her. Her head was going around with thinking about the robbery. She hardly noticed when she stumbled and fell and then got up again to start off as fast as she could.

Her brain swam trying to figure out what she should do. She knew she should obey Uncle Jack, and at the same time she felt she should call the sheriff. What if the men discovered Uncle Jack and killed him? She couldn't see why he had to stay there, why he couldn't come down and send the deputies up.

By the time she was back in town she was so completely exhausted that she could no longer reason out what was right and what wrong to do. Her only thought was to get home. She dragged herself up the steps of the house, pushed open the door, and without taking off her coat flopped down in the big leather chair and fell immediately into a nightmarish sleep.

CHAPTER SEVEN

JAMES BURN IS DISCOVERED

Annie was wakened long before daybreak by the sheriff's posse returning from the hunt for the robbers. Annie heard the noise in the street, and rousing from her sleep rushed to the window to see what had happened. All she could see were tired, drawn faces, lit up by the light from the lanterns. Evidently they had found no trace of the thieves, for their faces looked grim.

Annie longed to rush out and tell the sheriff all she knew about the robbery, but though her law-abiding mind told her to tell, her loyalty to Uncle Jack warned her not to. So, she stood at the window and let them pass, without saying a word.

Even though it was not yet morning, she knew there was no sense in going to bed. She had slept enough to get rid of some of her tiredness, but her body still ached and her head throbbed from the strain of yesterday. She found Sandy sound asleep under the stove. She had been so weary the night before that she had paid little attention to him. She was ashamed of herself, for Sandy had had a harder day than she.

He seemed all right. The men had not even wakened him as they went past. Annie was glad that he was getting a chance to rest.

She got a glass of milk from the refrigerator and drank it, not wanting anything to eat. She had had nothing since lunch the day before, but she was not at all hungry.

"If only Uncle Jack had come down with me! I'd feel a lot better knowing he was down here safe. I'm afraid the sheriff's men will find him up there and think he did hold up the train."

She wished she had somone to help her, someone to talk to, but this town that had looked so friendly had turned against her. There was no one she could trust.

When at last morning came, she trudged wearily down to the shoe store. Everything looked just as it had when they had left it Saturday. "That seems years ago," Annie thought as she looked at the neat rows of shoes. "Ever since I've been here things have gone wrong. I'm not superstitious but it looks as though I jinxed the place. I've spoiled a party, Uncle Jack's house has been robbed, there's been a train robbery. I certainly must be bad luck! And still maybe it's not me. I'm not the only newcomer to town and I know Halk is after Uncle Jack. He's the one that's doing all the damage."

She dusted the counters and looked over the shoes. "I can't even deliver these unless Uncle Jack comes

Annie Was Glad to Rest

back soon," she told herself, "and that will be the end of our delivery service. No one will trust us again. Well, there's nothing to be done about it. If they want their shoes they'll have to come for them."

Not knowing what to do with herself and too worried to hunt around for something to keep her busy, she stood at the shop window looking down the street. There was an unusual number of people up early this morning. Even the men who had been out searching the mountains had not gone home to bed. They stood around in little groups talking. Some of them passed from one group to another getting as many different stories as they could.

Among them Annie saw Mrs. Speedle and Mrs. Bolker. They, as usual, seemed to have more information than any of the rest, and the group around them kept increasing. Suddenly a familiar figure appeared in the street.

"So Mr. Halk's still down here," exclaimed Annie. "I thought sure he'd be up at the mine."

If Mr. Halk was mixed up in the robbery as Annie thought, he was playing a safe game. He mingled with first one group and then another. When he left each group there seemed to be a heightened tension and one after another of the people glanced at the shoe store.

"Leapin' lizards, he's telling them about Uncle Jack. I just know he is," thought Annie, but there was little she could do about it. Certainly now more than ever before people would doubt anything she had to say in defense of him.

"All I can do is sit here and wait," she complained.

And she had a long wait before anything happened. Halk disappeared from the street and little by little the people too disappeared, all headed in the same direction he'd taken.

"Now what's he up to?" Annie wondered, but it looked as though she weren't going to find out. She wanted to close the store and follow the crowd, thinking she could find out more that way than sitting in the shop doing nothing. Not one person had been in this morning. But Jack had told her to open up, and though she questioned his reasoning she would do what he asked her to do.

As she sat there wondering what she ought to do the door was pushed open by a young man that she had never seen before. He wore a vivid plaid suit and a still brighter flowered tie.

"Hey, little girl," he demanded, "where's Burn at?"

"So they've found out," Annie said to herself, but aloud she said, "Burn, I don't know any Burn."

"Oh, you don't?" he looked at her as though he didn't believe her. "Well, where's Boot then?"

"He's not here right now." Annie was giving out no information.

"Well, where can I find him? I want his picture

before the sheriff gets here. Come on, where is he?"
He held a five-dollar bill out toward Annie so that
she could see the corner.

Annie was getting angry. Evidently this was the
first of the newspaper reporters. "I certainly wouldn't
tell you if I knew," she told him. "Now get out."

But the reporter didn't get out, for the door was
suddenly filled with people. Annie had been so busy
with the reporter that she hadn't seen them coming
down the street.

At the front of the mob was the sheriff. Close beside him was none other than Mr. Halk. He did not
look as though he'd been out with the searching
party. While most of the men's clothes were wrinkled
and their eyes were heavy with sleep, Halk looked
as spruce as ever. He wore his gray flannel suit and
in his buttonhole was the inevitable fresh red carnation.

The sheriff was doing the talking. "Where's Boot,
Annie?"

"I don't know."

"Well, didn't he open up this morning?"

"No, I did."

"Well, where is he then? He wasn't out searching
last night."

"No, he had to go out of town yesterday morning.
He isn't back yet." Annie knew the story was doing
Jack no good, but there was nothing else she could

tell them.

"Where did he go?"

"I don't know."

Mr. Halk seeing that the sheriff was getting nowhere interrupted.

"Just a minute, sheriff, let me talk to her."

He turned to Annie. Annie was afraid of him, but she was not going to let him trick her into anything.

"Now see here, Annie, we know all about that uncle of yours. He's James Burn, the one that robbed the train twenty years ago."

"That's not so," cried Annie, but the people were well aroused and agreed with Halk.

"Now we're going to find him, and it would be a lot easier on him if you told us where he is. We're not going very easy on him if we have to spend a lot of our time tracking him down."

"I don't know where he is." Annie refused any more information. "If you want him you'll have to go find him. Besides, he's not the guilty one." She looked at the sheriff. "Why, you know he wouldn't do that, sheriff. He's lived here for ten years and never done anything wrong, has he?"

She might as well have saved her breath. The sheriff had been well convinced.

"He lived under a made-up name. He's a jail bird, isn't he?"

The crowd had been growing more and more restless. Now one of the women near the door happened to see her shoes sitting on the counter. She dashed past the sheriff and his deputies who were guarding the door.

"It's good I saw these," she called grabbing them, "I'd probably never have gotten them."

"Hey, you can't take those till you've paid for them," Annie cried, but the woman already had them and other people, seeing what she had done, followed her example.

"He's probably been gypping us all these years," said one as he knocked a whole row of shoes on the floor trying to get his.

"The sheriff will probably lock up the place and then no telling when we'd get them."

The mob broke through the guard and soon the store was packed. Once they were in, the sheriff could not stop them. Furious at having been fooled all these years they broke the shoe racks, pulled tools from their hooks, and destroyed the furniture.

The sheriff and Mr. Halk had been pushed back into a corner near the window. They talked together, evidently trying to decide what to do. Mr. Halk seemed to be doing most of the planning. Finally the sheriff called to his men. They shouldered their way through to him and Annie heard what they planned to do next.

"He's probably up in the mountains. Be careful;

he's dangerous. We'll go out to the edge of town and follow the mountain road. Howard, you and Joe go back along the railroad track to cut him off if he comes down that way. The rest of us will divide into two groups, one to search the mine—."

"Do you think that's necessary, sheriff," the authoritative voice of Halk cut in. "He wouldn't be apt to go there. He'd certainly guess that's the first place you'd look for him."

"Well, maybe you're right." The sheriff still had a mind of his own. "But I think we'd better look there anyway. There's plenty of places to hide money down in there."

Halk was not pleased. He scowled and Annie was glad to see that the sheriff had upset him. Finally the men started out, and the others, seeing that the excitement would probably be farther on, followed.

Annie knew that some way she would have to warn Uncle Jack. "The only way I know to get there is the mountain road," she thought, locking the door on the ruined shop. "And the men are going that way. The only chance I have is to get there before they do."

She saw them far down the street as she left the store, and decided that she could make better time and not be seen if she cut through back yards. Racing as fast as her legs would take her she jumped across hedges and dodged swings and wheelbarrows and clotheslines.

"I've got to get there first. I've got to get there first," she chanted to herself.

She would think of nothing but that until she reached the mountain road. Finally her way was blocked by a white fence that would take some time to climb, so she cut between two houses out to the main street. She had passed the crowd, but they were not far behind her. They saw her and started running too.

"She knows where he is, all right," she heard someone say.

Then the sheriff's voice came, "No, don't stop her. Just don't let her get out of sight. She'll lead the way for us."

Annie didn't know what to do now. She knew that run as fast as she could she couldn't lose the deputies behind her. The only thing she could think of was to lead them to the mine. If only Uncle Jack hadn't started down! If he was still hiding up at the mine maybe he would be safe, for if they once got to the mine there would be Ruff and the four other men as proof that Uncle Jack was not responsible for the robbery.

She got past the place where she had looked at the village. She climbed higher and higher, her legs growing stiffer and stiffer. But as she looked back she was glad to see that the sheriff had not gained on her. Many of the people had stopped at the edge of town, but most of the men still came on. She could still see Halk at the head of them.

As she rounded a bend she saw a lone figure coming down the mountain road. It was Uncle Jack. She doubled her speed to reach him. "Go back, go back, Uncle Jack," she cried. "The sheriff's coming." But he kept on toward her.

"Oh, climb up there and hide," she said as she spied a clump of brush growing on the side of the rock above them. "I'll keep going and get them past you."

"No, no, Annie, if they want me, I'll not run away," Uncle Jack insisted.

Just then the Sheriff and Halk appeared at the bend. Halk was the first one to spot Uncle Jack. "There he is, men. Get him!" he ordered, as though he himself were the sheriff.

Annie threw her arms about Uncle Jack to protect him, but gently he pried them loose. "It's all right, Annie. Don't worry."

But it was far from all right. The men quickly and not too gently bound Uncle Jack's hands behind him.

"What's this all about?" he asked.

"You're James Burn." The sheriff made it a statement rather than a question.

"Yes, who told you? That one?" Jack nodded at Halk. "What proof did he show you?"

"Never mind, he's got proof all right."

"Yes, that he stole from Uncle Jack's house," Annie

butted in.

Halk couldn't let that pass. "I haven't been near Burn's house."

"No but your pal Ruff has been, while you kept us away."

"The girl's talking nonsense." Halk turned to the sheriff. "He admits he's Burn. Isn't that enough?"

"Yes, of course, I admit it. What difference does it make? I've served my sentence, guilty or not, and because I was once in prison is no reason for arresting me now."

There was a growing undertone among the men. They had had two train robberies at Butternut and they were anxious to make someone suffer for it. The sheriff, though, was anxious for an admission of guilt —not just an arrest.

"You served sentence for embezzling. What about the train robbery?"

"I had nothing to do with that train robbery, but I can tell you who did."

"What are you going to do? Accuse Horace Gila again, as you did at the trial?"

"That's exactly who."

"That won't stick. Of course, you'd pick him when he isn't here to defend himself, and you can't lay last night's robbery on him."

"Isn't he here? Show me the proof that I'm James Burn—not the clippings Halk there showed you, but the original newspapers. You were sheriff when the trial was on. You remember the paper with the pictures of me and Gila together. Find that newspaper and I'll show you Gila."

Halk wouldn't let the sheriff listen to him.

"He's bluffing. He's just stalling for time. Come on, these men want to get home and get some sleep. They've been up all night."

The men agreed with him. He knew exactly how to twist them around his finger. The procession wound its way back down the mountain toward the town.

Annie tried to get a chance to talk to Uncle Jack, but his guards stayed tight to him.

She looked around at the men, wondering if among them was Horace Gila. There had been only one picture among the clippings in which he had appeared, and that one was just a courtroom scene. He was so far in the background that no one would be able to recognize him.

The men looked like grim monsters to Annie. Many of them had been rather friendly with her since she had come to Butternut. They had stopped in to visit with Uncle Jack and would talk to her too, much more so than the women did. Even since the disastrous party yesterday afternoon they had not turned against her completely, but now there was not a single friendly face. She was on Burn's side and that was enough for them.

"I've got to talk to Uncle Jack. If only one of the men would stick up for me! I ought to be allowed to talk to him!" Annie was getting desperate. "He must know who Gila is, and Gila is back of all this trouble. If he could only tell me which one is Gila! If he could just tell me what went on up at the mine."

There was no opportunity for her though. The men were taking no chance of losing their prisoner. He had got out of what they thought should have been a robbery charge twenty years before and they weren't going to let him get out of this one. As they came closer to town they closed in tighter and tighter about him, afraid that with the crowd pushing them he would try to escape.

Uncle Jack had no idea of trying to escape. He walked quietly with his captors. Annie knew that to run away from something would be the last thing he would do.

The people who had stayed in town saw the posse coming down the mountain and came to meet them. Mrs. Speedle, of course, was in front followed closely by Mrs. Bart.

As they neared the crowd Annie could hear Mrs. Speedle talking, as usual. She was taking credit for "having known it all along."

"I always said it was funny that he came to town without anyone knowing about him, and he never

Annie Ran After the Men

once got a letter from any place. And now this little brat that he has. Where did he get her? There were never any letters came to him beforehand. She couldn't have just dropped out of the sky."

Everyone was so used to her talking that they paid little attention to it. The important thing right now was that Burn had been caught. There was talk of a lynching and of taking justice into their own hands, but the sheriff, as anxious as he was to see Burn sentenced, would not tolerate disobedience to the law. He ordered men he could trust to form a circle about Jack and with the people pushing in on all sides to get a look at the robber, the procession moved into town and down to the jail. At least it was called a jail, though actually it was a shed behind the sheriff's office. The circle of men had to break up to get up the steps of the building, and Annie seeing her chance slipped under an outstretched arm and was at Jack's side before anyone realized what she was up to. She hugged him to her, his face pressed close to hers. For a second he stayed so, unable to speak. Then, his lips hardly moving he whispered, "Watch Ruff, not Gila. You'll find—"

He tried to say more, but the sheriff pulled him up toward the door.

Annie knew that another chance would not come soon again. She turned sadly back to the street. The crowd made way for her, acting as if she were something they didn't want near them. She walked across the street, and blinded with tears, stumbled on to the shoe store. She still had the key and she fumbled for the key hole. Why she had bothered to lock the store she didn't know, for it seemed that everything that could possibly have been ruined was scattered over the floor.

She stumbled over a shoe which no one had claimed and fell down beside the little stool she had used as her own. Torn between fear and anger she stayed there until her tears had spent themselves and she could began to plan. There seemed little enough that she could do, and still she knew that if Uncle Jack were to be saved she was the only one who could do it.

"If only I could call Daddy," she thought. Whenever she had been in trouble before he had either been nearby himself or had sent someone to help her, but now she was all on her own. There was no place to turn for help.

"I've just got to find a way out. I've just got to."

But that was far easier said than done. Where could she start? "There isn't a single person in town I can trust," she told herself. "Everyone else thinks Halk is a hero, and as long as they back him they won't believe me."

It was then that she got her first good idea. There *was* one person in town who didn't believe in Halk.

Annie didn't know her, but maybe she could help. Yes, of course, the librarian. Halk had indirectly caused her plenty of grief. The women had all been most indignant with her when she could find no book by him.

"At least it's worth trying," decided Annie, wiping her tear-stained face with her handkerchief. "I don't know how she can help, but maybe she can."

There was no one in the library when Annie got there. Annie found Miss Jens back behind a stack of books, dusting and sorting.

"There hasn't been anything doing around here," she told Annie after Annie had introduced herself. "No one seems to be reading these days."

Annie knew why not. Mrs. Bart set the style for the town and if Mrs. Bart didn't read, the town didn't read.

Annie didn't quite know how to start asking her questions.

Finally she asked, "Miss Jens, have you been in town very long?"

"Very long! I've lived here since I was born. Why? That's a funny question to ask."

"Well, I wondered if you remembered the other robbery."

"Yes, of course. I was only in grade school then, but I remember the big fuss about it. Burn and Gila were the two promising young men of the town and

all the girls were crazy about them," Miss Jens told
Annie.

"Didn't you recognize Uncle Jack when he came
back?"

"Why, no, Annie, I didn't. No one did."

"I think that's queer," Annie puzzled.

"Well, ten years can make a lot of difference in a
man. He had black hair then, and no mustache, of
course."

"Do you suppose anyone would know Gila if he
came back?"

"I don't know, Annie. What are you trying to say?"
Miss Jens was puzzled at Annie's insistence.

"Uncle Jack says Gila's around here, and if he is
it's funny that no one has seen him. Isn't there someone around that might be Gila?"

"No, almost everyone here has lived here all their
lives. There's only Jack Boot, and you and Mrs. Bart,
but she lived in Raymont before she was married,
and of course she's not a man anyway. Then there's
Ruff who used to live here and— Annie, you don't
mean you think *he* is Gila?"

"Ruff, oh no, I'm sure he's not."

"I didn't mean Ruff. Halk! You know, he might be.
He's about the right height."

"Do you think so? That's what I hoped. Isn't there
any way you'd know?"

"I don't know how, unless—wait a minute." She

darted back to her desk and consulted a notebook. "Come on, let's go down cellar."

Annie followed willingly. Miss Jens sounded as though she were as anxious as Annie to find out about Halk. After all you couldn't blame her. In a small town the librarian is looked up to, and Halk had managed to turn everyone against her, just by saying he had written a book. The stairs were dark and gloomy. Down in the basement were long shelves filled with bound newspapers and old worn-out books. Miss Jens walked down the aisle until she reached the volumn she wanted. She pulled it out and blew the dust from it. The light looked even dimmer with the cloud of dust she had stirred up. She propped the volume against the edge of the shelf and leafed through to the section she wanted, then systematically she scanned each page from top to bottom. Finally she was rewarded. The headlines of the robbery that Annie had seen appeared. Each following page seemed to have more information. Most of it Annie had already seen, but occasionally there was a clipping that somehow had failed to get into Uncle Jack's box.

"I know just what I'm looking for," Miss Jens informed Annie. "There was a big picture of Gila the day he testified against Burn. It must be here because Mrs. Bishaw, the librarian before me, was very careful about filing papers. We have every copy since the

Butternut paper started."

She slowed down as she came to the accounts of the trial. "It ought to be the next day," she decided, and she was correct.

On the first page of the next issue was a two-column spread of Gila. He was standing on the steps of the courthouse in Raymont which was the county seat. He was very good-looking, even Annie who disliked him without even knowing him had to admit that.

"It does look like Halk, doesn't it?" she asked the librarian, hoping that there really was a resemblance between the two men.

"I don't know. I just don't know." Miss Jens, like Annie, wanted to believe it, but she couldn't be sure. "If only he didn't have that mustache now it would be easier."

But there was one bit of incriminating evidence that neither of them noticed at first glance. They were so busy looking at his face that they had slipped past that bit without even noticing it. Suddenly Annie, who had her head bent close to the picture trying to memorize every detail, let out a whoop.

"Look at that! Doesn't that look like Halk?" she almost shouted.

Yes, there in his buttonhole was a fresh carnation.

"Yes, it does, Annie, but just that wouldn't be proof. Just because both Gila and Halk wear carnations is no sign they're the same person."

"Well, can't you remember, Miss Jens? Did Gila always wear flowers?"

"Yes, that's the funny part of it. He did."

"There, see! That's certainly proof enough for me."

"Now look, Annie, be sensible. You've got to be able to prove something before this does you any good. Even if Halk is Gila what good will it do you?"

Annie realized Miss Jens was being sensible and yet any small ray of hope was better than nothing and this seemed like a good strong ray.

"Can I take that paper?" she wanted to know, but Miss Jens shook her head.

"The newspaper files have to stay here," she explained, "but if you could get some other proof—enough for court, then we could get a court order to use this if you still need it."

This news was rather discouraging. Annie felt just about back where she started. Miss Jens knew how she felt. "Cheer up," she counseled. "Now that we are almost sure that Halk is Gila, probably other things will clear up too. Why don't you trail Halk? Would that help any?"

"Gee, Miss Jens, you're swell." Annie astonished the librarian who couldn't see that she had said anything out of the ordinary. "I forgot all about what Uncle Jack said. He said 'Watch Ruff, not Gila' and here I've been watching Halk all the time."

"But what did he mean? Ruff hasn't enough brains to back anything like this."

"I don't know what he meant, but that's what he said. I'm sure of it. 'Watch Ruff, not Gila' and if Halk is Gila I've been watching the wrong one."

CHAPTER EIGHT

ANNIE FINDS A CARNATION

Undoubtedly Uncle Jack knew what he was talking about. Certainly in the time Annie had watched Halk he had done nothing to help her find a solution to this mystery. Perhaps she should trail Ruff, but where was he? The last she had seen of him he was up at the mine with the robbers, at least Annie was sure they were the robbers.

She had thanked Miss Jens and promised to report back to her as soon as she could, and Miss Jens had also promised that she would try her best to think of something to help Annie.

Annie had made a trip to the jail, hoping to be allowed to see Uncle Jack, but the sheriff would not let her in. Halk was beside the sheriff and it looked as though he were helping to engineer the whole business.

"There's no use in my going back there until I can show some proof. If I could have that picture, maybe they'd believe Halk was Gila, but somehow I bet he'd still make them believe that he had nothing to do with it."

She hunted the streets for the big black car and for

154

Ruff, but there was no sign of him. Finally she decided the place to go was the place she had last seen him—up at the mine.

"That's where Uncle Jack found out whatever he did find out, and that's where I'd better go."

She planned her trip to the mine very carefully this time. She packed a good substantial lunch just in case things were too interesting to leave to come back to town. She took the lantern and the clothesline. The good stout rope Jack had taken with him must have been left up near the mine, for she had not seen it when he was arrested.

There was one important change she made in this trip. Feeling hardhearted and a little frightened at having this trip to do all alone, she banished Sandy to the cellar and closed the door behind him.

"I'd like to have you with me, Sandy," she explained to him through the closed door, "but I don't dare risk you going after Ruff again. You'd give us away, and besides, no telling what Ruff would do to if he caught you again."

Sandy, of course, greatly disapproved of the arrangement, but though he barked and whimpered from behind the closed door there was nothing he could do about it, and Annie would not change her mind in spite of his pleadings.

She said good-by to him once more and closed the outside door behind her. As she went along the street she tried to keep out of everyone's sight. It was early afternoon and the street toward the mountain seemed deserted. She glanced at front windows as she passed them, hoping that no one would happen to glance out as she went past. Certainly Annie going toward the mountain with a rope and a lantern would be a topic of conversation all through the village, and it probably would not take long to get to Halk's ears. Not only Jack's freedom but her very life probably depended on getting out of town unseen. She was thankful that Jack lived near the edge of town. Though it seemed to take forever, she knew it was a matter of a couple of minutes getting past the houses. Once out of town, she hurried as fast as she could to get around the bend of the mountain road where no one could glance up from the town and discover her. To her knowledge, she got out safely. If someone had seen her, she had not seen them.

The path from here on was so well known to her by now, the place where she could stop to look at the town, the turn where she had met Uncle Jack coming down, the towering cliffs on each side between which one got his first view of the mine—all of it was so familiar that the road should have seemed short, but it seemed to go on forever. Perhaps it was because around each turn she feared she would find Ruff or one of the other robbers. Each curve was a new campaign to be mapped out in her mind before she tried it.

There were so very few hiding places along the road. If anyone were climbing down she would most certainly be caught. But though she momentarily expected to see a foot appear around a sharp curve, she saw nothing. She reached the straight road that led directly toward the shaft house and moved off to the side where the scrub pine would partially hide her. She moved steadily closer to the house, but still there was no sign of life.

"If I can only get around to that knothole I first looked in," she thought, "I can probably see what's going on inside."

There was nothing to stop her from getting to it. All her caution seemed wasted, for though she hesitated at each step and thought out her next one carefully, no one challenged her, no one even appeared to investigate. At last she could put her eye to the crack and peek in. The room looked exactly as it had that first day. There was no sign of a living thing inside. Annie waited and waited expecting to see a light appear in the shaft and a figure swing up over the edge of the ladder, but nothing happened.

Finally, tired of waiting, she put down the rope and the lantern so that they would not hinder her or make a noise, and as stealthily as she could she crept to the door, pushed it open, and looked inside.

The room was empty. The only sign of its having

been used were footprints in the dust on the floor, and even they were blurred as though a new coat of dust had already started to cover them. Annie went in, walking carefully in the latest footprints in hope hers wouldn't show. She knelt down at the shaft and as on the first day peered over the edge. No bats greeted her today. Evidently they had been driven to some new hiding place, afraid of all the light and activity that had invaded their home.

The ladder was still there. It was too dark to see down to the first level, but Annie listened and could hear no movement below her. Finally, feeling hesitant but somewhat safer, she went back for her lantern and rope. With the lantern lighted she could see down to the first passageway. The round of the ladder had been replaced. Whoever had fixed it had used an old piece of wood, probably hoping that if anyone investigated they wouldn't notice the new addition, but it was a poor job of fixing. The hammer marks were too fresh, and the wood had not been worn smooth the way the other ones were.

Evidently there was no one around. Annie hesitated about going down into the pit for fear someone would appear as Halk and Ruff had done that first day. She certainly couldn't expect her luck to hold again. If they came down this time, they would undoubtedly catch her. But how else could she find any proof, any clues to help her? Resolutely she started

She Peered Down the Shaft

down. Each moment she was afraid she might hear the sounds above that told of the men returning. She reached the first level, but everything was just as she remembered it. She wandered up and down the passageway, but saw nothing at all to show that someone else had used the mine.

Seeing that she was getting nowhere here, she went down the next ladder. All the light down here had to come from her lantern. Not a bit of the dim light from above filtered down to this level. This was all new to her too. There is a spooky feeling in being under the ground that she didn't like.

"Where can they keep their stuff," she wondered as she crept quietly along the passageways and still discovered no sign of life. "They must have some food, and probably some tools, and the money ought to be here some place, too."

But there was nothing. It was as though she had dreamed she saw men here. Suddenly a disheartening thought came to her. Perhaps the men and the money had both gone. Annie knew that the sheriff was taking no chances and had had the roads guarded as soon as she learned of the robbery. Since they hadn't found the money yet, probably the roads were still guarded. "But they must have got out some way," decided Annie, "and if they did how am I ever going to get any proof to help Uncle Jack?"

Discouraged with this new idea, and yet determined to cover every bit of ground before she gave up, she kept on along the passageways, wandering this way and that in the creepy underground rooms. Finally she found a spot where the passageway was blocked with a big pile of rock. The cave-in probably. It looked as though there had been some recent digging. Annie could not be sure. Perhaps those rocks had lain there for the last twenty years with the marks of picks on them. She wanted to believe that they were fresh marks, but she couldn't feel very encouraged. Finally she made her way back toward the ladder. Though she gave every bit of ground another glance she found nothing at all.

"I might as well give up," she had to admit to herself. "There just isn't anything to see down here."

She started up the ladder once more. When climbing a ladder everyone knows one should look up to the top, not down, but part way up Annie stopped to take a last look at the passage below. She flashed her lantern around so that she could see in every direction. As she brought it back close to her so that it would be easier to carry, she saw a spot of a different color below the ladder, right against the stone to which the ladder was fastened.

Hoping against hope that this was what she wanted she climbed down again. Yes, it was. There again Halk's vanity was getting the best of him. It was a withered red carnation. A red carnation. Could it belong to anyone but Halk? No one else around Butternut wore flowers in his buttonhole. Carefully Annie picked it up and put it in her pocket. Here was proof that Halk was interested in the mine. Still wondering if the robbers had cleared out, but a little cheered at her find, she made her way back up the ladders to the ground floor.

Still there was no sign of life.

"It looks as though they didn't plan to come back. There's not a sign of anything left here. I guess I might as well go back down. I guess I can't find Ruff up here. I don't know where to look for him now."

She gathered up her rope and her lantern and though she was not hungry, opened her sack and picked out a sandwich to eat as she went down the road.

Suddenly she heard the rumble of a car in the distance. The robbers hadn't left; they were coming back! That gave her a chance to find out what she wanted to know. She scooted back to her hiding place in the scrub pine. It still seemed the best place around for hiding. She crouched there, her half-eaten sandwich in one hand, her lantern in the other, waiting for the car to appear. Certainly whoever was coming was not coming quietly. If they were afraid of being seen they would be far more careful than this.

As the car came into view Annie discovered it was Halk's car. Exactly what she had hoped for! Yes, Halk was driving, but the rest of the people in the car looked familiar. As the car stopped and they climbed out and stretched, Annie recognized them—it was the sheriff and three of his men.

"Now what will I do?" thought Annie. "This will look worse than ever for Uncle Jack if they find me here."

She made herself as small as possible, hoping that she would make no motion that would give her hiding place away. As the men came closer she could hear their voices.

Halk was still protesting about searching the mine.

"Though why he should worry about it now," thought Annie, "I can't see. Unless I didn't know where to look, there's nothing to find down there."

Halk was still arguing. "It would be the last thing he'd do—put it here. Probably those confederates of his have it all out by now."

"They couldn't get it out," the sheriff reminded him. "The roads have all been guarded since that first night, and they couldn't have gotten away from there in half an hour."

"Well, we won't find anything here!" Halk sounded stubborn. He banged the car door behind him.

They disappeared behind the shaft house and Annie worked her way to her knothole to spy on them. The deputies were the first to go down. Halk stayed at the top calling occasionally to the rest of them below. With no one around to see him he had a very pleased smile on his face. He glanced around at the room as though he were giving it a final checkup. Annie was thankful that the sheriff and his men had not even noticed the footprints on the floor. By this time she was pretty sure that they had walked over hers enough so that they wouldn't show.

Halk stood around peering over the edge of the shaft occasionally, but the men must have been out of his sight. He lit a cigarette and strode back and forth across the floor impatiently waiting for them to return.

Finally a light appeared in the shaft and Halk again peered over the edge. The light grew brighter and brighter and Halk stretched out a helping hand as the first man reached the top and climbed up off the ladder.

"Did you find anything?"

"No, not a thing."

"Well, I warned you. He's smart enough to pick a better place than this."

"Someone has been down there though."

Annie saw Halk start. "Has there? How do you know?"

"Someone's been working at the cave-in."

"What good would that do anyone?"

The sheriff himself looked puzzled. "I don't know. I can't figure it out."

"Oh," Halk reassured him, "probably just some kids playing at mining."

"No, I don't think so," one of the deputies piped up. "Someone who knows how to handle a pick worked on it."

"Well, if the money's not here, there's no use worrying about it. Say, do you suppose there would be any use opening the mine up again?"

The idea was a new one to the villagers, Annie could see. They looked at each other in surprise.

"Why, I don't know," the sheriff pondered. "As far as I know they were getting pretty good hauls out of the mine until Burn got the money. I don't think any of the bankruptcy had to do with the amount of ore."

"I think I'll look into it." Evidently Halk was going to put his finger in another pie. "It might not be a bad investment. I don't know much about mining, but I suppose if I could find a good manager I'd be all right."

The men looked at each other. Butternut had been a far more prosperous town when the mine was going. You could see them figuring what it would mean to them personally.

"I think that sounds like a good idea," said one of the fellows. "You should be able to get plenty of labor from around here, and the railroad down in the valley used to do quite a business hauling ore."

"Who's owner now?" Halk wanted to know. "Is what's his name, Gila, still owner?"

"Why I would guess so, but you'd have to see one of the lawyers in Raymont about that. No one around here even knows where he is."

"Why, oh why, doesn't someone discover that that's who Halk is?" Annie mourned to herself. "Wouldn't you think someone would notice the resemblance?"

"Well, I suppose there'd be no harm in getting a little crew down here to explore, and see what they think about opening it up. Do you suppose I'd have to get permission to look into it that far?"

"I don't see why. After all this hasn't been used for twenty years. No one would know the difference. I don't see any harm in it."

"Well, come on, let's get going. We've seen everything there is to see around here."

"Just a minute. Let's take a look around outside. Just maybe he was smart enough to hide it around the house instead of in it."

"Oh, oh," thought Annie. "Where do I go!"

There was little chance for her to get away. The sheriff called to the rest as he led the way out the door. "You two go around that way. We'll go this. Let's hurry it up. That's a long trip back."

Annie retreated toward the back of the building but there just was no place to go. The sheriff found her first.

"Say, what are you doing up here?" he asked, surprised at finding her.

Annie decided there was nothing to be gained by showing them she was frightened. "I came up searching."

"Did Boot send you up here? I knew you shouldn't have been allowed to talk to him." The sheriff was anything but pleased at finding her.

"I came up here because I thought this would be the place the robbers hid the money," Annie retorted. "I came up for the same reason you did."

"How often have you been up here?" Halk's eyes were blazing with anger and behind that Annie saw fear. She wished she had enough proof to make him really afraid.

"I've been up here about as often as you have," she told Halk, and though this told the sheriff little it frightened Halk more than ever.

"If I don't get shut up now, I'm going to have to spend all my time side-stepping him," thought Annie. "He'll never let me alone now."

Halk's question seemed very unimportant to the sheriff. "Have you been down in the mine? Were you there before we got here?"

"Yes, sir."

"What did you find?"

Annie searched through her pockets and pulled out the wilted red carnation. "This." She held it up to the sheriff.

It was obvious to everyone to whom the carnation belonged. They turned as one toward Halk. Halk was crimson with fury.

"Where did you get this?" he demanded.

"Just below the ladder on the second level," Annie answered.

Halk turned to the sheriff. "Why that's a downright lie," he stated. "I haven't been down there. You know it."

For the first time the sheriff looked as though he might be doubting Halk's statement. Halk saw the look too.

"Why, she probably picked it up here after we went into the mine." Everyone glanced at his lapel and he did also. A fresh red carnation was still in the buttonhole.

"Or she picked it up on the street in town. I know I lost mine yesterday. I noticed it wasn't there when I got back to the hotel."

Still the men said little. Halk's mouth grew grim.

"At least he's worrying a little," thought Annie.

But Annie's troubles were not to be over that easily.

"Come on, Annie, you'd better go back to town with us," the sheriff decided. He picked up her lantern and handed it to one of the men. "Now let's hear about this," he said after he had bundled her into the car and they had started off down the road. "What were you doing in the mine?"

Annie told him just what she had done after she got up there. There was nothing that would harm either her or Uncle Jack more than they already were by her admission that she had searched through the mine.

"And you didn't find anything?" the sheriff questioned.

"Nothing but that carnation," Annie admitted.

When they reached town he was still not through with her. "Come on into the office with me," he commanded and there was nothing for Annie to do but precede him up the steps. Halk was planning to follow, but the sheriff called to him.

"I won't need the men any more for a while. Take them home, will you?"

Halk looked ready to refuse and then thought better of it.

"He's got to keep on the right side of the sheriff," thought Annie.

Just Annie and the sheriff were in the office. It looked as if he had planned this purposely. Annie was frightened, but she didn't need to be, for he motioned to her to sit down on one of the rather uncomfortable chairs in his office and he sat at his desk facing her.

"So you're trying to find something about that robbery. Didn't Boot do it?"

Annie wondered if he were trying to trick her into admitting something. "I'm sure he wouldn't do it," she told him. "Where would he get someone to help him? Even Mr. Speedle said he didn't get any mail, and until Sunday he hadn't been out of town for close to a year."

Her theory was convincing. "Yes, I had thought of that too," the sheriff bit his lip in concentration. "The engineer said that none of the fellows looked at all familiar, and he's been going through here so long that he knows most of the people around here. Those fellows must have come from out of town. Besides I doubt if there were five men unaccounted for at that time of night."

"Well, neither Halk nor Ruff were down at the station," Annie led him on.

"So you've picked out Halk as the guilty one. Did you know who Boot was before the robbery?"

Annie couldn't follow this abrupt change from Halk to Boot. However there seemed no harm in admitting it now. "Yes, I found a box of clippings— the same clippings Halk showed you, I bet."

"Umhum." The sheriff seemed interested. "How did he get them?"

Annie told all the details of that morning and when she finished the sheriff astonished her by saying, "And now you think Halk is Gila."

Annie's eyes opened wide. The sheriff smiled at

her. "You aren't the only one who goes hunting," he said, opening his desk drawer. He pulled something out and handed it to Annie. It was the same picture that Annie had seen in the library.

"Got that down at the newspaper office. Jack said something about looking at it, so I took his advice even if I did believe him guilty."

"But then why don't you arrest Halk?" Annie wanted to know. "If Uncle Jack isn't guilty and he is, why isn't Uncle Jack out?"

"Hold on, youngster. What proof have we against Halk? Just because he's Gila doesn't prove he's guilty any more than your uncle being Burn proves him guilty."

"But you arrested Uncle Jack," Annie argued.

"Yes, he was not around town that night. He was up in the mountains; he admits that. He's an ex-convict. It's circumstantial evidence, but enough to arrest a person on. We haven't anything against Halk."

Annie was astonished to find the sheriff, if not exactly on Uncle Jack's side, was at least not sure of his guilt.

"Why don't you accuse Halk of being Gila?" she wanted to know.

"There's no reason for it now. I have proof here. I can use it any time I want to. I'll hold off a while yet, and don't you say anything."

Annie didn't have to make a decision as to whether to promise or not, for the door opened without any knock beforehand and Halk came in.

"Well, well, still got the little spy here," he commented. "What are you going to do with her?"

Annie was no longer afraid to meet him if there was someone else around. She knew that the sheriff had no idea of ganging up against her with Halk. Even in front of Halk he refused to bully her.

"Well, I think I'm sending her home to get some rest right now."

"You know I think this would be an interesting case to look in to," Halk had evidently done some figuring since he had left them. "Burn only had a sister didn't he? Did she get married?"

"Why no, she died the year after Burn was convicted."

"Well, who is this Annie then? There couldn't be any nieces or nephews either. What relation are you to him?" he turned to Annie.

"I'm not any relation. He took me in because I needed a place to live."

"See, that just shows how he's been pulling the wool over your eyes all these years. 'Uncle Jack' indeed. Picking up a beggar off the street and introducing her as his niece!"

To Annie, mad as she was, his indignation seemed faked. He was putting on an act, and like all amateurs

Halk Walked into the Room Without Knocking

he was overacting.

"The place for her," recommended Halk, "is the county orphanage. I'm sure the village wouldn't want her corrupting their children."

"Well," soothed the sheriff, "there's plenty of time for that. If Burn is convicted I suppose that's what we'll have to do. But I don't think we should decide that until after the trial. There's no harm in letting her stay at Boot's place until things are settled one way or another."

"I think you're mistaken." Halk assumed all the dignity he could muster. "You'll find the town won't approve of having this—this hoodlum running loose. No telling what she'll get into all by herself."

"Well, nevertheless, whatever the town thinks, I intend to give her a chance until the trial is over."

Annie wished she dared thank him, but all she could do was smile. There was no sense in making Halk any angrier than he already was. He stalked out without as much as saying good-by to either of them.

"Well, that's that. Don't worry, Annie. You won't have to go to that orphanage if I have anything to say about it. Now go on home and get some sleep. You look all in."

"Golly, I don't know how to thank you," Annie began, but the sheriff cut her short.

"You've had a pretty rotten welcome from this

village. I hope I don't have to do anything to make things worse for you than they are. Now go on home and get some rest."

CHAPTER NINE

DOUBLING THE PROFITS

Annie was tired, but she certainly didn't feel like sleeping. Although now there were two people in Butternut on her side, she still saw no hope for Uncle Jack. The only thing today's work had accomplished was to bring things out in the open. Halk knew now that she suspected him. He would make it harder than ever for her to find out anything about his affairs.

Slowly she walked over to the library to report to Miss Jens, but the library was closed. Annie hadn't realized how late it was getting. She knew the thing to do was to go home and get some rest as the sheriff had ordered her to do, so that she would be ready to start the next day. She didn't know what she would do, but something would just have to turn up.

"I suppose I've got to go home," she told herself, "but I hate that house without Uncle Jack in it. It seems so empty." She thought of Sandy locked in the basement and knew how anxiously he would be waiting for her.

"Neither of us have had much of a meal these last few days," she discovered. "I guess that's the first thing to do—get some hot food into us. Maybe I'll feel

176

better then."

She opened the front door carefully. After that horrible feeling when she had found the house all upset, she hated to open the door. No telling what one would find inside. The house, though it had that queer empty feeling houses get when no one has been in them for a day, was just as Annie left it. She could hear Sandy whimpering down in the cellar, and she hastened through to let him up.

He was certainly glad to see her. He leaped at her and licked her face, and though she told him to get down and behave himself, his joy at seeing her did her good. Relaxing was what she needed most.

Feeling a little comforted, she washed and changed her dusty clothes.

"I'm just going to forget all about Halk until I get through eating. Even thinking about that man makes me lose my appetite," she told Sandy. That was not an easy task she had set herself, for he popped into her head every few seconds, and she would have to force herself to forget him.

She spent some time getting her meal, and then took as long as she could eating it. She dreaded the long lonesome hours ahead of her, and she tried everything she could think of to cut them shorter. She took her time washing and drying each dish, polishing it a great deal harder than was necessary.

Just as she was emptying her dish water she heard

someone enter the front door. Sandy too pricked up his ears, but made no move to go after the intruder.

Annie, her heart pounding, called, "Who is it?"

"Don't be frightened Annie. It's just me." The form that came through the kitchen door was certainly nothing to be afraid of. It was little Miss Jens.

She had come for a definite purpose, that was certain. She wasn't wasting any time in visiting.

"You don't want to stay here alone do you, Annie?"

"Oh, it doesn't bother me; I'm used to being alone."

"But with all the things that have been happening . . ."

She stopped short as both of them heard the door opening again. They waited to see who it was. A man's voice called from the parlor, "Annie."

"Yes, I'm out in the kitchen," Annie called back. It sounded like the sheriff to her. He, too, when he came into the kitchen, looked as though he had something very important to tell Annie. Seeing Miss Jens he stopped short.

"I didn't know anyone was here. I'll come back later."

"Oh no, it's all right. Miss Jens knows all about Gila."

"Well, this isn't about Halk—it's about you. It looks as though you were going to have to go to the orphanage."

"Oh, no!" Annie paled as she heard it. "But I can't.

How could I ever help Uncle Jack then?"

"I think that is the idea, Annie. You know who's back of this. Halk has all the people set against you."

"Yes, Annie," Miss Jens broke in. "That's why I wanted you to come to stay with me."

Annie looked from one to the other, puzzled. She didn't know just what she could do.

"I'm afraid even that won't work." The sheriff didn't like to have to tell them, but there was nothing else to do. "Everyone took it for granted Annie had a legal right in staying with her uncle, but now that people know she wasn't related to him they would be sure to take her away."

"Yes, but couldn't I adopt her, or take out a guardianship or something?" Miss Jens tried to find a way out.

"I suppose so, but it would take time. Annie would have to go to the orphanage in the meantime."

"I can't do that," Annie's face was panic-stricken. "I can't be shut up where I can't help."

"I wish I knew what to tell you, Annie." The sheriff was sincere in trying to help. "It almost looks as though the best thing for you to do is go away from Butternut. If you don't want to go to the orphanage— and I don't blame you, it's a horrible place—you'd better get out of town before the people force me to act."

"And leave Uncle Jack? I couldn't do that."

"There's just nothing else for you to do."

Miss Jens too wanted to find a way out for her. "We can give you money to go on, and maybe after this blows over you could come back."

"But what would happen to Uncle Jack in the meantime?"

"We'd just have to trust to luck. I'll try my best to prove he is innocent," the sheriff promised, "but I can't fool you. It doesn't look too promising."

"Well, I just won't go and leave him, that's all." Annie was stubborn. "I'll find some way."

"Come stay with me tonight anyway, Annie," Miss Jens repeated her invitation. "Perhaps before tomorrow we'll think of something."

"Thanks, Miss Jens, you've been awful good to me, but I think I'd like to stay here one last night anyhow."

"I'm afraid the townspeople will be here tomorrow morning, Annie. They're right as far as the law goes. I can't do anything to stop them if they ask me to take you," the sheriff warned.

"Don't worry, sheriff. I'll try to figure something out, and if I do get taken to the orphanage, I wouldn't blame you."

Though they argued with her, trying to talk her into taking some money from them for train fare and leaving on that early morning train, she refused to listen to them.

"If Uncle Jack needs me, I'm staying."

When Annie came to Butternut Jack had felt that the only way to keep her there was to make her feel she was needed. He had been right. Now even the thought of an unpleasant orphanage could not drive her away.

After the two friends were gone she tried to puzzle out some way to stay.

"I just won't go to that old orphanage," she told Sandy. "I've had enough of orphanages in my day. Lots of them are O.K. but I seem to hit all the bad ones, and from what the sheriff said this one isn't a very good one."

She looked around the house trying to plan what she would do. It would be impossible for her to plan what she would do. It would be impossible for her to hide in town so that they wouldn't find her.

"I know what we'll do, Sandy," she suddenly spoke to her dog. "We're going back up that mountain. If the robbers aren't using that mine any more, why can't we use it?"

The more she thought about the idea the better she liked it. The sheriff had searched the mine already. He wouldn't be apt to make another trip up there. Halk's gang had probably made all the use of the mine they intended to, for it had been well cleared out. It looked like a good safe hiding place.

"It'll be kind of uncomfortable, but I guess we can

manage, can't we?" Annie asked, and Sandy "woofed" his agreement.

Then there was no time for sleep.

"We've got to be ready to go early in the morning. I'll have plenty of time to sleep after we get up to the mine," thought Annie.

She opened the cupboards and hunted for canned food to take along. She was sure Uncle Jack would not mind her taking the food. She found an old blanket, too, that would come in handy. Her greatest worry was about light. She'd have to have light down in the mine, and a lantern needed refueling occasionally. Finally she hunted up all the candles she could find around the house. They were ones left over from Christmas mostly. She found several white ones and three partly burned red ones. She added a small frying pan to her equipment too.

"I can think of so many things we could use," she told Sandy, "but I know we just couldn't carry them all. The thing is we've got to take what we need most."

Even so when she finished she had a good-sized pack. She wrapped all the canned goods and the frying pan and candles up in the blanket and then slung it over her shoulder to try the weight. She staggered doing it, but once it was up she thought she could manage it all right. She put the bag down near the door and refilled the lantern.

"I don't know just how I'm going to carry everything," she complained to Sandy. "I've only got two hands and it looks as though I ought to have a dozen."

She settled down to rest for a little while.

"We'll have to get going early. We don't want anyone to know where we've gone." She laid her plans carefully. "I wish we could tell Miss Jens and the sheriff what we've decided to do. They'll worry about us, and so will Uncle Jack if they tell him, but we can't take a chance. If they don't know, then there's no one here who could tell the townspeople about it."

Long before daylight she roused Sandy and together they ate their last meal in the little white house. Annie cleaned everything neatly and took a last look around before she shouldered the heavy pack and started out. They trudged up the stony road paying little attention to what they were seeing.

"I feel as though I'd walked up and down this mountain so often that I could do it blindfolded," Annie sighed. "I'll bet I've worn off at least two inches of the mountain going over it."

The distance had become shorter between home and the mine. If it hadn't been for the load Annie had to lug, it would not have taken long to climb, but the pack grew heavier with each step she took and often she had to set it down to rest.

"I'm sure we didn't take more than we're going to

need," she worried, "but I feel as though we could
live a year on this pile."

Sandy had nothing to hinder him. He galloped on
ahead and then raced back to Annie only to start off
again. He got to the mine building before Annie even
came in sight of it. He stood at the doorway where
Annie could see him, his legs stiff and his hair
bristling.

"Oh gee." Annie had had so many things go wrong
that she couldn't do anything but set her pack down
and stand still. "There's someone there."

Sandy left his place at the door and raced back to
her. "Is there someone there, Sandy?"

Sandy was grumbling low in his throat. "I'll bet it's
Ruff or Halk," decided Annie. "There's no one else
that Sandy hates that way." She dragged her equipment over to the hiding place in the pines and edged
carefully to her knothole. She could see no one above,
but there was a light coming up from the shaft. Near
the shaft were several big boxes that had not been
there before.

"What do you suppose that is?" Annie wondered.
The light came brighter now and she knew that whoever it was was climbing the ladder to the ground
floor. She kept a tight hold on Sandy.

"You keep quiet," she warned. "Don't you dare
make a sound."

Sandy's ears were pricked up, but of course, he

She Edged Carefully to Her Knothole

couldn't see through the knothole. He stood there just wanting the chance to go after whoever was there. Annie watched a hand appear on the ladder and then a face. It was no one she knew. Right behind him came another figure, and this one was Ruff.

He stayed on the ladder until the first man had carefully lifted one of the big boxes onto his shoulder and then he disappeared. The first man pulled one of the boxes close to the opening and then went down again far enough so that he could ease the box off onto his shoulder.

"They're treating that stuff awful carefully," thought Annie. "I'd like to know what's in it. It can't be the gold, because they could bang that around without hurting it."

The two men made several trips back and forth until all the boxes had disappeared down into the mine.

"Maybe Halk's really thinking about opening the mine," decided Annie, "but he couldn't get fellows up here that fast. He just mentioned it yesterday."

The light seemed fainter now. It would get a little brighter occasionally, but no one seemed to be coming up the top ladder.

"Do you suppose I dare go in?" Annie asked herself. "I think I could get out before they got up far enough to see me."

She crept cautiously to the door and peeked in to

watch the light for a moment before she decided it was safe to go in. She looked over the edge of the shaft. There were a couple of boxes down in the passageway below her, but evidently the rest had been taken down to the next level. As Annie watched, the light grew brighter and the man she had first seen came up the second ladder. Annie pulled her head back from the edge and put an arm around Sandy who had followed her in, so that he wouldn't be tempted to bark. She could hear the man below. He had got to the boxes and was swearing softly as he pulled and tugged to get one of them on his shoulder. Though Annie could not see him, she could tell just what he was doing by the sounds he made. Gradually the noise lessened and the light grew fainter and again cautiously Annie stuck her head over the edge. Everything had disappeared. The view below was exactly what she had seen the first day.

"Well, the robbers are here," she whispered to Sandy, "but what do we do now?"

She could hear what sounded like a faint rumble of voices below and the sound of someone working at the rock. "I can't see what they could be up to unless they're trying to hide the gold in that cave-in part. But there doesn't seem to be anything much to stop them from getting out with it. Why should they bother to hide it?"

Suddenly she discovered that the voices were getting clearer. Hastily she and Sandy retreated quietly through the door and back to their knothole. By the time Annie had her eye to the hole the first man was appearing from the shaft. He was followed by three others, all of them strangers to Annie, though one looked like the man who had been with Ruff the night he had kicked Sandy. The men stood around blinking a little in the brighter light.

"That's a heck of a musty place," crabbed one of them. "I'll have a case of rheumatism before I get out."

"Oh, quit the grouching," one of the others cautioned. "When you get through here you can afford to have rheumatism. This is the best thing the boss has worked out yet."

"Yah, who'd think a little hick town like this would have anything in it for us," added one of the others.

"Well, if the boss hadn't known the ins and outs of it, we wouldn't be doing so hot. He sure has a way of wrapping people up, don't he?"

The light in the shaft had grown bright again and this time Ruff appeared.

"How soon can you have her set, Buck?" he asked the one who had been with him the night of the robbery.

"Guess it ought to be O.K. by tomorrow afternoon. Do you want I should blow it before the boss gets here?"

"No, you wait for him. He's the one that gives the orders. He'll want to be here when you get her open."

"I wish to heck he'd hurry up," the one who was afraid of rheumatism complained. "I'm sick of this cold and wind up here all the time."

"Give him time," Ruff ordered. "He's not going to hurry this up and have that hick sheriff down on our ears. You can manage this climate for a week. When we've got the dough you can spend the rest of your life in Florida if you want to."

"Boy, this has sure been luck though, hasn't it?" the men seemed very pleased with themselves in spite of their physical discomfort. "Getting two gold shipments in one haul. I keep wondering how long our luck will hold."

"That reminds me, Ruff, shall one of us stay at the shack?"

"Why?"

"Well, all that money's under the steps."

"Oh, forget about it. No one's going to bother it. The boss has given 'em plenty to keep them interested down in the village. They won't be up here again."

"O.K., but don't blame us if it disappears. I ain't crazy about hanging around there all alone; it's spooky."

"Well, go on, get going. You don't want to waste time standing around. We're all so anxious to get out of this place," Ruff seemed to have some authority.

"Sure, we're going to get something to eat and then we'll be back. You get back here as soon as you can."

"Well, probably not till tomorrow. The boss says people are beginning to ask where I go every day. We'd better play safe."

"Bring him back with you then, so that we can blow the thing."

Ruff went down the road to town, and the four others started in the opposite direction across the ravine and along the narrow path to the miner's camp. Annie had to edge around the corner of the building as they followed the path so that she wouldn't come in their view.

"If they've gone for lunch, I ought to have enough time to do some investigating," she told Sandy. "You stay right here until I get back."

Sandy wagged his tail, but he sat down as though he understood what she said. Taking her lantern she went into the mine.

She climbed down the ladder to the first passage, but there had been no changes made there. All the activity had been farther down. When she reached the second level she found picks and shovels strewn on the passage floor, and near the cave-in the boxes had been piled. Annie could see no label telling what was in them, so she pulled one toward her, balancing it against her stomach while she peered over to see what was on the other side.

"Leapin' lizards, that's dynamite!" she gasped, easing it back onto the pile. "No wonder they were treating it so carefully."

She walked carefully around the boxes. She had no desire to bump into them accidentally. The cave-in itself was interesting. Someone had been working on it. Those pick marks that she had noticed before had increased in number.

"I guess that's the way they get ready to set the charge," she decided. "I wish I could remember more about mines. That's what he meant when he said it would be ready to blow tomorrow.

"I don't see what good opening up the cave-in will do them."

She climbed back up to the ground level and thought she agreed with the fellow who didn't like the feel of the mine. She went back to Sandy and then they got out enough lunch to satisfy them until the men came back. Annie had had so little sleep and the noon sun was so warm that before she realized what was happening she was sound asleep. When she awoke the sun showed her that she had slept some time. Sandy was curled comfortably beside her.

"Golly, do you suppose we missed the men?" She had intended to keep a close eye on them. She left Sandy guarding their provisions and crept back to her knothole, then into the shaft house and to the shaft.

Far below she could hear the sound of a pick and occasionally the sound of a voice as it yelled to some-one else. Daringly she crawled down the first ladder and peeked on down to the second level. She could see no one, but the voices were clearer now. Evi-dently they were not all working, for Annie thought she heard the sound of only two picks. The other two were trying to carry on a conversation over the noise that echoed and re-echoed around them.

"Ain't it funny how he waited twenty years to get his dough?" one voice was saying.

"Yah, and then to get a chance at another haul at the same time. That's playing luck."

One of the picks stopped for a minute and a new voice said, "It isn't luck with him; it's good figurin'. You'd probably have come back inside a year and got caught doing it. He's waited so long that every-one's forgotten that he existed almost."

"Anyway," one of the first speakers resumed, "this makes a nice take for us, him letting us in on both hauls."

"Sure and with that Boot down there taking the rap no one's going to be hunting us after we leave here. We're safe as heck."

"So that's it!" Things were getting clearer. "The first gold shipment couldn't be found because it was down here all the time. That cave-in must have been accidental then and now Halk's going to get the money he stole twenty years ago."

She climbed back up, afraid that one of the men might decide to come up and she wouldn't be ready for him. She had no desire to be caught on the first level as she had been the day Ruff and Halk had come exploring.

Up on the main floor again, she glanced back but there was no sign of them coming. There was no sense in staying where they might find her. She retreated to the spot where she had left Sandy. The late afternoon sun did not warm her the way the noonday sun had. She pulled the blanket from around the food and wrapped herself up in it.

"If there were some way I could trap them in there," she concentrated. "Then the villagers would have to admit that Uncle Jack wasn't behind this. Maybe after they're gone I can think of a way."

The wind grew more and more chilly. She pulled the blanket tightly around her, but the wind seemed to come right through.

"I'll have to use the mine to sleep in tonight. I can't stay out here. And then if they come back and catch me in there I'll just be a goner."

But she had no choice in the matter. She'd certainly freeze outside. She'd just have to trust to luck that she would wake up and get out before the men came back. Evidently they were sleeping over in the miners' cabin. Finally the men appeared at the door of the shaft house. They stood there arguing about something, but Annie could not hear what it was. At last the one whom Annie had dubbed the "scaredy cat," the one who didn't like the cold, started off toward the path. He yelled back at the rest and that Annie did hear.

"Come on," he called. "You don't want to have to go over the narrow path after dark. You haven't got too long to make it."

The other three followed more slowly, but the first one didn't wait for them to catch up. He, at least, didn't intend to walk the narrow path in the dark.

CHAPTER TEN

THE BEST-LAID PLANS

Left alone Annie tried to make plans. She decided to leave most of the food where it was, hidden among the pines. She took the lantern, her rope, the blanket and enough food for their supper with her.

"We don't dare make a fire in there," she told Sandy. "They'd see it, or even if we could clean it out they could smell it tomorrow. Then they'd start hunting."

A cold supper was not very interesting, but Annie felt as though her day had been quite successful, and pleased with herself she wandered about the room as she ate, hoping that there would be some way of trapping the men. She couldn't see any possible way of trapping them in this part of the mine. It would have to be down farther. "Or maybe I should have gone over to the miners' shack. Maybe I could have shut them in there."

But it was too late for that now. Besides she realized just closing the door probably wouldn't be enough to hold five husky men anyhow.

"I've got to find some better idea than that," Annie told Sandy. Sandy too had been rummaging around the room. The only thing that interested him was the chain of footprints, some of which belonged to Ruff. He grumbled at them, but Annie warned him that he'd just have to be quiet. He sprawled out then at the top of the shaft, one paw hanging over the edge.

"I'm going down there," Annie informed him, "and don't you get into any mischief while I'm gone. You stay right here."

She lighted her lantern, deciding that would be easier to carry than the candles, and with the rope tied to her belt as she had seen Boot fix his, she went down the ladder. Sandy watched her carefully but this time he didn't try to follow her. When she got to the first level she waved back at him and then disappeared down into the lower part of the mine.

The men had left their picks and shovels where they had used them. The dynamite boxes were still untouched. The only thing that had changed since noon was the pile of rock that blocked the passageway. They had chipped and dug here and there, making little places to set the dynamite sticks. Annie looked at the pile. "If I could only find a way to get that money before they did. Then I know where the other is, and if I took it back to town they'd have to let Uncle Jack go."

Now, though, it was not just a matter of getting Uncle Jack free. The criminals must be caught and punished.

"I guess what I really ought to do is go back to town and get the sheriff. He believes me now, I think, and he'd come back with me." That did seem the sensible thing to do, but Annie began thinking of the way Halk could wrap the townspeople around his finger.

"It would be just our luck to have him see me, and before I could get the sheriff to come, he'd have me headed for the orphanage. Or he'd talk the people into believing I was leading the sheriff on a wild goose chase and he wouldn't dare come."

It looked as though she would have to play a lone hand. Now was the time to test herself, to find how clever she could be. Right now she felt very dull and stupid. She couldn't see any way of keeping the men down in the mine.

"I suppose I could swipe some of their dynamite and set off a charge in the upper passage while they were below, but I don't know anything about it. The whole mine might cave in, and they'd really be buried. However much trouble they've caused I couldn't do that to them."

She went back up to the first level and looked into all the sections hoping she would get an inspiration, but it was no use. Finally tired out, and knowing that she'd better get to sleep so that she wouldn't over-sleep the next morning, she started up the top ladder. Sandy looked down at her as she climbed up.

"Boy, it's good these ladders are strong. I'd sure hate to fall off one of them," she said, shaking the ladder to test how strong it was. Sandy didn't like that one bit. He barked worriedly at her until she clambered up over the top and sat down beside him.

"It's all right," she informed him. "It's solid."

Curious about it, she looked to see how it was fastened. Big iron staples had been fixed around the two uprights and driven into the wood flooring. Holding the lantern over the edge Annie lay down on her stomach to see where else it was fastened. The only other fastening was down at the bottom. It looked as though two more pieces of iron had been used against a board placed between the beams of the windlass.

"I'm going back and look at those again," Annie said, sticking her feet down over the edge. "I think, just maybe I've got an idea."

She inspected the ladder closely, first at the top and then down at the bottom.

"If I can find a way to get those things out, I know what we can do," she told Sandy. "If only I had something to work with."

All thought of sleep was forgotten. In spite of having had no rest for two nights, she seemed to have a great deal of energy left. She took the lantern outdoors with her, to see if there weren't something in her supplies that she could use to pry the ladder loose. But she had not planned for such an emergency. The

She Inspected the Ladder Closely

strongest tool she had was her knife and that would surely break under the strain.

Shivering from the cold wind that howled across the mountain top, she went back into the shaft house.

"No luck at all," she thought. She puckered her brow in concentration, and Sandy too looked as if he were thinking hard.

"What'll I do now?" she asked him, but of course he had no answer for her.

"I've just got to find a way. That's our only chance and I'm not sure even then if it will work. Maybe I can't budge that ladder after I get the fastening out. But at least I could try."

She started down it once more, inspecting the staples on the way down. They were in there tight; there was no doubt about it.

"And if I don't find something soon, I'll never get them loose before they come. I've got to do something tonight, because they're going to open the passage tomorrow and then they'll probably get out right away. They'll have all the money then."

Her lantern cast a narrow circle of light around her.

"This is like going down in a dungeon," she called back to Sandy. "I'd sure hate to be trapped down here." She went down the second level ladder and glanced back at the towering rock around her. "Or like being buried alive," she shivered.

She walked down to the cave-in and stood still

staring around her, her mind concentrating on her problem. She certainly couldn't use the dynamite or the boxes it was in. The shovels were no good, but maybe those picks could be used.

"If the end is small enough to work under the staple," she pondered, "I think I can use them."

She carried one to the stairs with her. It was impossible for her to climb with both the lantern and the pick in her hands. She had to have one hand free to hold on to the ladder. Finally she decided to take the lantern up first and then come back for the pick. Going back for it, though, was harder than ever, for the passageway caught little of the light from above. She groped around in the dark to find where she had put the pick and then carrying it gingerly she started up once more.

She stayed down at the bottom of the first ladder and started prying at one of the staples. Sandy leaned far over the edge to see what she was doing.

"This is going to take a long time," she told him. "Those things were put in here to stay. And I'm none too good working this pickax. It's so big and heavy. I work so hard just holding it up that I don't have much force left for the prying."

Though it was a long slow process she could see a shiny spot of metal where the iron had pulled away from the board.

"At this rate it'll take me all night. I hope the other

ones aren't as stubborn as this one. I don't know whether my light will last."

She hated to use all the oil from her lantern. If she had to go down in the mine again she didn't want to go down in total darkness.

"It's good I brought those old candles along. I'm going to switch to them," she told her dog.

That meant climbing up and going out into the night again to rescue them from her supply base among the pines. This time though she was glad of the chance, for the struggle with the ladder was tiring.

She brought back a can to set the candle on, because she intended to take no chance in letting the robbers find signs that someone had been there. If the candle were down on the ground there couldn't help but be telltale spots of wax to warn them.

She set the can at what seemed an advantageous spot and lighting the candle she dripped some of the hot wax onto the can and stuck the candle upright in it.

It was far harder working by candlelight than it had been working with the lantern. When she blew the lantern out, the candle seemed very dim in comparison. It took a while to get used to it. The flame would not stay steady. The wind from the musty passages played havoc with it. It fluttered and danced like something alive. One second it died down to nothing only to shoot up to a brilliant cone a second later.

"And to think that once upon a time that's all people had to read with. I can't even work by it let alone read," she grumbled, but though she said she couldn't work by it, she kept right at it. When the candle leaped high with light the shiny spot on the iron showed that it was growing longer. Gradually she could feel it pulling away, and at last she had to be careful that it didn't pop out and throw her off balance.

"I'd hate to get in the way of the point of the pick," she decided. But the staple behaved itself very nicely. It gave a sucking sound and came loose, clattering down to the floor at Annie's feet.

"One down and three to go," she told Sandy who was still peering over the edge of the flooring at her. "Maybe this one will be easier to do too, now that I know how to go about it."

It did seem easier. Though it refused to budge at first, Annie wedged the pick point between it and the wood farther and farther until finally it too gave up.

The top ones were far more ticklish to work on. She stood part way up the ladder and pried, at first, but she couldn't balance herself and put any force on the pick at the same time. At last she climbed up beside Sandy and lying on her stomach she held the pick over the edge and worked. It was a most uncomfortable position. She had to get up and rub her

neck and back several times before the first peg had
budged at all.

"The first part is always the hardest. When it's once
out a little way then it'll come easily," she informed
Sandy.

Sandy had been having an easy time of it. While
his mistress had been up and down the ladders a
dozen times, while she had been pushing and pulling
at the ladder fastenings, he had flopped flat near the
shaft so that he could keep an eye on her and still
take a nap every few minutes.

Now he was rested and rather bored watching her
work. He stood up, stretched, and wandered about
the room. Then he disappeared into the night. He
went out and back several times, and Annie was so
absorbed in her work that she paid little attention to
him. She finally got one side free and started on the
last one. Sandy was still there then, because she talked
to him about how to work on that last peg.

"If I just go on working it might come loose all of
a sudden and the ladder would fall down into the pit.
Then they couldn't get down, and neither could I.
I've got to find some way to be sure it's safe while
I'm working on it."

That wasn't as hard a problem to solve as she
thought it would be. She had her rope with her. What
could be better? She tied the end of it around the
top of the ladder and then wound it several times

about one of the windlass supports.

"There, that should hold it." She surveyed her handiwork with pride. "Now there's no chance of it's getting away from me."

She pushed and pried at the other fastening and suddenly the ladder swayed free from all restraint.

"So far, so good," she thought, "but now comes the tricky part."

She still had to be sure the ladder was really loose. Kneeling beside the hole she grasped the sides of the ladder and pulled it straight up. It came all right.

"It's going to be heavy to move, but I think I can do it." She let it slip back, grateful for the easing of the weight.

"The next thing is to get it back where it was, and steady enough so that they can get down it."

She fitted the staples back into their places at the top. Just like a nail that has been pulled out and then put back into the same hole these slipped in easily.

"Now I've got to get those back in the bottom part too, and I don't like the idea of going down it."

She tested the top step with one foot, keeping her weight on the ground. The ladder wobbled under even that little weight.

"I don't trust it," she said to herself, "but I've got to get back down there. They'd never get down it the way it is now."

She unwound the rope from the support and tied

it around again using a good solid knot to hold it tight. The other end she tied around her waist.

"I feel kind of like a mountain climber, but I'd rather be safe than sorry. Now if the ladder does tip I can catch hold of the rope and pull myself back up."

Thus armed she tackled the ladder again. It felt anything but steady under her, but though it swayed and scraped against the side of the shaft, it held. Down at the bottom she stuck the other two iron prongs back in their places and shook the ladder. It still was none too firm, but using the side of the pick she forced the iron in a bit tighter and the ladder felt as though it would hold even a fairly heavy-set man.

"That's that," she thought. "And if I have luck to-morrow there will be five less criminals at large by sundown."

She picked up her candles and everything else that she had used. "The pick had better go with me," she decided. "I may need it to pry out the bottom fastenings again. They won't know it's gone until they get way down to the cave-in, and by that time I hope I'm all finished up here."

She carried all her possessions back to her hiding place. Sandy was not in sight. The night was so very dark that he might be close by and yet she wouldn't be able to see him. She didn't know how long he had been gone; she had been too busy to notice him. She called softly, hoping he might hear her, but he didn't appear and she was afraid to call any louder. There wasn't a great deal of chance that the men would hear her even if she yelled her loudest, but she wasn't planning on taking the slightest risk of having her plans go awry. She prowled down the road a way. She should have been sleepy, but the excitement and suspense were too great to let her rest. For a while she stayed in the house, but as soon as she saw the first few streaks of gray that herald the morning she headed back to her hideout. She certainly was taking no chance of anyone seeing her. She was beginning to worry now about Sandy. Of course, he could take pretty good care of himself, but she hated to think of what would happen to him if he got in the way of the robbers.

"Poor Sandy; he's been anything but a help these last few days. Every time he gets in the way of those fellows makes things harder than ever."

Daylight came, and Annie lunched once more on the cold things she had in her store. She wished for a hot breakfast, for the air was still frosty and she was none too warm, but after a night of work even the food she had tasted good. It was queer that Sandy had not shown up to get his food. It wasn't often that he missed a meal. The sun appeared behind the mountain shining through the mist like a giant orange. Annie wanted to get to a place where she could watch the trail from the miners' cabin, but she could see no place that was hidden both from the trail and from the road. She remembered that Ruff was due back some time during the day, and it was just possible he would want to get out of town early before anyone saw where he was headed.

The safest place, she decided, was right where she was. There was no sense in spoiling her chance now. She was well chilled and there was nothing she would like better than to run along the road to get warmed up, but that too was taking too much of a chance.

It was not until the sun had burned away the mist from the mountain top that she heard voices a great way off. She was sure it was the men coming across the ravine, but her view was blocked by the house. They came closer and finally Annie could hear "scaredy cat's" voice complaining again.

"I'll bet it's the cold he's complaining about." Annie who had been out all night had little sympathy for him this morning. "I'll bet he'd think he had pneumonia and hardening of the arteries and half a dozen other things if he had to stay out here."

She stretched her legs to ease them, and rubbed some of the numbness from them.

"Once they get in sight I'll have to sit pretty still so they won't spot me. Any wiggling I want to do I'd better do now."

They seemed to take an awfully long time to get across the ravine. Annie remembered that path. At first it had been hard, but it grew easier as it went downward.

"I can't see why it takes them so long. There's nothing to stop them along there."

But they were taking their time. At last they appeared coming up over the ridge, but they were walking slowly and visiting along the way. Today they seemed in better spirits. They seemed to be joking and having a good time together. There was even some pushing and shoving directed at "scaredy cat," who looked as if he had been suffering agonies going over the narrow trail. They stopped outside the shaft house to look down the road toward town and one of them walked far enough along the road to see down to the bend. Finally they all went back to the house and after more discussion went inside.

Annie didn't know whether to chance going to the house or not. Perhaps they were just inside and had not yet gone into the mine. She wished that Sandy would show up. He worried her staying away like this, and no telling when he would come back. He'd probably head right for her and the fellows would see him.

"I want him to come back, and yet I wish he'd stay away till those fellows have gone down into the mine," she thought, wriggling around to limber up her cold muscles before she tried to go to the shaft house.

"I've got to be able to run fast just in case I get caught, and I don't think I'd ever be able to as cold as I am."

After all her wiggling around she was still stiff and frozen. "I'm not getting any better by just sitting. I might as well get up and try it."

Her legs felt like tree stumps and she was sure she clumped along loud enough for everyone inside to hear her coming. She got to the knothole finally and took a look to see if the coast were clear. The men were still in the room. No one seemed to be making any start to go down into the mine itself.

"That's funny." Annie was puzzled. "I thought they had to get that dynamite all set for today. They don't act as though they were ready to work."

She didn't have to wait long to find out what it was all about. The one who had been with Ruff seemed to boss the others around a little and it was he who was doing most of the talking.

"There's no sense our going down there until he gets here. All we've got to do is place the dynamite and set it off. That won't take more than half an hour."

"Yah," said the "scaredy cat," "you sure padded the time when you told Ruff yesterday."

"Well, I didn't want the boss up here and us not ready. He'd of blasted blue blazes out o' us if we weren't ready when we said we'd be. This way he'll think we worked extra hard."

Annie Saw That the Men Were Still There

"Sure, and if you'd told him we'd be ready this morning we could have cleared out of here by noon. I don't like these roads at night."

That of course was "scaredy cat." The rest let out loud guffaws of laughter at him, but he was planning on taking good care of his own skin.

"How do you suppose he ever got to be a criminal?" ran through Annie's mind. He certainly didn't have any of the usual bravado that criminals have. He looked like a timid unsuccessful storekeeper or perhaps a piano teacher. "You sure can't tell by looks," she decided. "Halk looks like a big businessman, and Ruff kind of looks like a farmer. That one that's bossing the rest around now might easily be a mailman. He even looks like one that brought our mail in New York."

She amused herself thinking about the men and wondering how they had happened to become criminals.

"I'll bet the only thing every one of them thinks about is money. I can't see how people can do anything under the sun for it. Money can be the greatest thing in the world. It can relieve suffering and right wrongs the way Daddy uses it, and then it can make wrongs and make suffering the way the war lords and the criminals use it. Sometimes I wish there were no such thing."

The men were getting restless and uneasy. Waiting

around in an empty house, with no place to sit and nothing to amuse them was getting tiresome. They probably felt pretty nervous too, the crime so near and yet not done.

The sun was getting higher and Annie was beginning to get warm. She wished that something would hurry and happen. She was getting tired of waiting, fearing they would notice that something had been done to the ladder.

At last the one who seemed to be engineering the blasting admitted his boredom.

"I'm getting tired of waiting around here," he told the others. "I guess I'll go down and see if everything's all right."

The others were glad to have something to do. They followed him toward the ladder, and one after another disappeared over the edge. Annie held her breath as each one passed from view. She knew that just about then they would be looking at the place where the ladder was fastened and if they noticed that the staples had been tampered with they would be searching for whoever had done it. They got down to the foot safely though. One of them had lighted his lantern when he reached the level and was holding it for the others. Soon the light from it became fainter and Annie guessed that it would be safe for her to go in.

"I wish they'd waited for Ruff," she thought, although a moment before she had been anxious for them to get started. "I can't very well trap them now. I want all of them, but so many things could happen and I wouldn't have any of them. I wish Halk and Ruff would get here."

She stood at the top of the shaft and watched the dim light way at the bottom.

Suddenly she heard a voice right at the foot of the second ladder.

"It isn't here," it called back to the rest.

"What isn't here?" wondered Annie, and then she remembered. She had one of their picks.

"I'll see if it's above," came the voice again, sounding as though its owner were already part way up the ladder.

"I'd better get out." Annie made a beeline for the door.

Just then she heard someone racing up along the road. She ducked back of the building just in time. The person coming up the road was Ruff, and he was certainly coming! Annie couldn't help peeking around the corner to see the spectacle. She had not imagined Ruff could run so fast. But he had a reason for stepping lively. Behind him, almost at his heels, came an infuriated Sandy, snarling and lunging at him, but never quite reaching him.

"Good Sandy," Annie whispered to herself. "At last he's getting his chance."

The two covered the distance to the house in no time. Sandy seemed to gain a bit at every step. Ruff bounded through the door, giving it a push as he passed it, hoping probably that it would close, but Sandy gave it no time. He was through it before it had a chance to swing shut. Ruff was at the top of the ladder when Sandy caught him. Evidently he had no gun today, for his only defensive effort was another vicious kick. Unlike the one of two nights before this one didn't land. Sandy was wise to him and side-stepped in plenty of time. While Ruff was getting his balance, Sandy caught his pants leg. Annie had come right into the doorway to watch the battle. Ruff was too intent on getting out of Sandy's way to notice her. She heard a ripping sound and then Ruff got his legs down over the ladder. Sandy spat out the piece of trouser leg that had come off in his mouth and went for Ruff again, but he had no chance to get another hold before Ruff got beyond his reach.

Annie could hear him scrambling breathlessly down the second ladder, and before he had reached the bottom he was yelling for help.

"Now," thought Annie, "if I want a chance, now's the time."

CHAPTER ELEVEN

ANNIE GETS HER MEN

She raced back to her supplies, wishing she had brought them with her when she had first started back to the shaft house. She grabbed the coiled-up rope and the pickax she had taken. Dragging the ax behind her over the uneven ground she headed back to the shaft.

Sandy was still standing over the ladder grumbling at it. No one was in sight below though Annie could hear excited voices from the second level. She fastened her rope from the ladder to the upright as quickly as she could and crawled down the ladder to loosen the staples. They needed a little prying out, and Annie set to work with the pick. She expected any moment to hear the men storming up the second ladder to get rid of Sandy.

She heard "scaredy cat" say, "There's been someone around all right. Let's go ahead and blow her and get out." He sounded panicky.

Ruff's voice came in too. "The boss said he'd bring the car in an hour. He's getting his stuff ready to get out in a hurry. Have you got everything all set?"

Someone answered but Annie couldn't hear what

216

he said.

"Let's not wait for him then. Let's blow it and then we'll just have to load up when he comes."

Annie worked at the prongs, but she had pushed them back harder than she had realized. Now she had to be additionally careful because she didn't dare make any noise.

"Look," said Ruff, "what about that dog? We've got to get him out of the way. He probably won't even let us up out of the mine."

"Well, let's worry about him when we get to him, not before." That was a new voice to Annie, but then there were two of the men that she had never heard speak.

"We've got to go up though." That was "scaredy cat." "We've got to see if there's anyone around before they blow the thing."

"That's right. We don't want to walk into the arms of anyone coming up to inspect."

"Well, come on, then," Ruff sounded disgusted.

"More likely he hates to get near Sandy," thought Annie.

"Have you got your gun? Let me take it. I'll get rid of the hound."

"Hope you have better luck than you've had so far," the one who had seemed to be placing the dynamite said.

"That cur isn't going to bother us any more, I can

tell you that."

Annie had the bottom prongs loosened and was up to the top again. She knew they were coming. She hurried with the top staples. They were easier, and soon she had them free, the ladder holding by nothing but the rope around the windlass support. Unwinding the rope from the upright she took up the slack and began to pull. At first nothing happened. Then she could feel the ladder coming free. It was still close enough to the bottom for them to reach and hold on to and she could hear the voices getting closer. Sandy, seeing what she was trying to do, came running to help, and together they pulled and tugged at the unwieldy load. The ladder hung slantways across the opening and then finally slid through.

"There!" she cried, dropping the rope with a sigh of relief. "That does it!"

There were indignant cries from below and then a bullet went whizzing harmlessly straight up to the roof. From below it would be impossible to hit anything that was not directly over the hole.

"Gee, Sandy, was I glad to see you." Annie had time to think, now that the robbers were safe below. "I thought sure you were lost and all the time you must of been waiting for Ruff to come. Whew! You got him here just at the right time. They'd just discovered their pick was gone, and I didn't know what I was going to do."

She wished she dared look over the edge to see what their faces looked like, but she didn't dare risk a bullet whizzing up at her instead of at the ceiling. She listened to the outraged voices below for a moment and then turned back toward the road leading to town.

"They'll keep warm enough till I get back if they keep that language going," she told Sandy. "The air's certainly hot with it now."

She wished there were some way she could fly down that mountain. It was going to take forever to get down to the sheriff even if she could run all the way. Happiness did seem to give wings to her feet though. She bounced along as though she had been having more than enough rest for the last few days. Sandy, too, proud of his encounter with Ruff, who for once had not bested him, seemed as frisky as a young lamb.

"I hope they don't find a way out," Annie, who had thought of every possible thing they might try and decided that all of them were impossible, worried. "They can't throw a rope up 'cause there's nothing that they could lasso up there, and there's no way for them to climb up. I guess they're safe there all right. It's just too bad that Halk isn't down there too, but I'll bet the sheriff gets him before he can skip town."

The long downhill grade faded away in no time at all. "That's the fastest time we've made yet," said

Annie. "If we keep it up, we'll think that's no harder than going upstairs in a house. Maybe we can make real mountain climbers of us yet, Sandy."

As she entered town people looked at her curiously. She had forgotten that she was due for a trip to the orphanage, and that probably everyone thought she had run off. Now in spite of her happiness at having caught the robbers, she looked with distaste at the places where she had been so ill-treated.

As she got down to the main part of town, she met more and more people. Some of them stopped and stared at her. She could feel them trying to decide what to do.

"If they want to get the sheriff after me, I can save them the trouble," she told Sandy, "because I'm going after the sheriff."

They passed the shoe store and Annie glanced sorrowfully at the ugly mess that had once been so carefully cared for. Before she had gone much farther she felt rather than saw someone keeping step with her. Sandy too had noticed it and turned to look, but had paid little attention. Without slowing her pace, Annie turned her head to see who it was. It was Mary Lou Bart, mimicking her movements.

When she saw that Annie had seen her, she started chanting, "You're going to get sent to the orphanage. Your uncle's a jailbird."

Annie had no time to turn on her. "There'll come a

day," she promised herself. "Someday she won't be so high and mighty."

She wasn't going to let a brat like Mary Lou bother her, and she wouldn't waste her precious time on her either. It would be fun to see her face when she learned who really was the thief, but that news was too good to let her be the first to hear it. Annie increased her speed until she was almost running. She hoped to leave her tormentor behind, but the faster Annie went, the faster Mary Lou went, and her derisive chant kept time with her running. If Annie had not hated her before, she had her fill of her long before she reached the sheriff's office.

She raced up the steps with Sandy tight at her heels, and that's one place Mary Lou didn't want to follow. She had never been a favorite of the sheriff's, and he was not afraid of her mother as most of the towns-people were. She stayed clear of him and worked her wiles on those she knew would give her her own way. She stopped at the bottom of the steps and ventured no farther.

Without breaking her speed Annie plunged through the door and came to an abrupt halt.

Thank goodness the sheriff was there, but he was not alone. Halk was with him. When the sheriff saw her he gave a glad cry as though he had been worried about her. Halk didn't react that way at all. He turned white. Evidently he had been sure Annie was out of the way for good. His mouth dropped open in astonishment, but he quickly recovered his dignity.

"Well, sheriff, the tramp came back. Now's your chance. You'd better take care of that little matter before you lose her again."

The sheriff wasn't interested in what Halk had to say. He had eyes only for Annie.

"Where have you been? What happened to you?" he pelted her with questions, not giving her time to answer them.

Annie, her eyes sparkling with excitement, finally managed to get in an answer to one of his questions. She was answering him, but she turned toward Halk as she did it.

"I've been up in the mountains," she announced.

If Halk had been pale before he bleached another shade now. He didn't need three guesses to know what that meant. He was a good hand at camouflaging his feelings, though.

"Look," he turned to the sheriff, "you'll be busy for a while now. I'll come back later."

The sheriff was anxious to hear what Annie had to report and didn't stop his departure. Annie tried her best to make him see that he should hold on to him. Halk went out the door and then Annie exploded.

"But he's the one. You can't let him get out. He's the boss of the gang."

The sheriff still refused to be worried.

"He'll stick around. If he does go, he can't get very far. His car's supposed to be all fixed up. He had it in the garage yesterday so that everything would be ready for today. I figured maybe he intended to pull out. So, the spark plugs haven't been put back yet."

Annie laughed. "Well, even so he can get farther than the ones I've got."

"Ones! How many have you got?" He was more interested in that than how she got them or where they were.

"Five," she told him, "counting Ruff."

Then he was more astonished than ever. A girl catching *five* hardened criminals didn't seem possible. As soon as she told him where they were, he started gathering up his equipment. Going to the door he called across to the barber whose shop was just opposite the jail.

"Hey, Jed," he bellowed, and the door across the street opened. The barber stuck his head out, and still bellowing the sheriff gave him instructions. "Get your stuff closed up over there. We've got the train bandits."

The bellow was loud enough to attract others. Beside Jed in the doorway appeared the bank president, his round front draped in a white barber's cloth, and one cheek covered with soap suds. When he heard what all the uproar was, he used the cloth to wipe the suds from his face and clumsily tried to find the strings at the back of his neck to untie it.

Mary Lou had been hanging around outside. She made a beeline down the street as soon as she heard the news, probably heading for her mother to tell her the gossip. Like all news, once started it spread like wildfire. Soon there were more than enough men to help.

The sheriff was not idle while the men were collecting. Telling Annie to hurry up, he headed for the garage. Halk was still there. His face was white with rage or fear, Annie could not decide which; he was playing the last cards of what was pretty sure to be a losing game.

As he saw the sheriff he tried to calm down and be his normal polished self, but in an emergency the polish wore very thin.

"Come on," the sheriff ordered him, not saying a word of accusation. "We've found the bandits."

"You have?" Halk was still trying to brazen it out, evidently hoping that his connection with them had not yet been discovered. "Why did it have to happen just now? I guess you'll just have to count me out this time. My car isn't ready yet."

"Come on in mine." The sheriff was pretending friendliness. "We won't need yours."

"I think I'd better wait." Halk tried hard for a logical excuse. "It was supposed to be ready early

"Come on," the Sheriff Ordered

today, and I want to see that it gets done. Where did you find the robbers? Maybe I could come along as soon as the car's ready."

"There's no sense waiting for that." The sheriff could think of excuses too. "Why this garageman is one of my best deputies. I couldn't get along without him. He'll have to leave your car and fix it when we get back. Come along."

All Halk's excuses were of no avail. He was worked carefully toward the car, and before he knew what was happening found himself in the back seat next to Jed, the barber. Annie had noticed that the sheriff and Jed had a whispered conversation and now she knew what it had been about. Jed's hand stayed close to his gun, and at any move from Halk he pulled it part way from its holster.

The sheriff assigned the front seat of his car to Annie and Sandy, and glancing back to see that the rest of the deputies were following he stepped on the gas and raced for the mountain road. If Annie had admired the skill with which Ruff and Halk had driven that road, she had to admit that the sheriff was an even better hand at it. The narrow curves and high ledges passed in a blur. He did not ease his foot on the accelerator until he brought the car to a grinding stop at the very entrance to the mine.

Annie, fearful that she had overlooked something and that the men had found a way out, had the car door open before the car had slid to a standstill. She was across the space between car and house in one bound, even beating Sandy who came close behind her.

There was not a sound from the shaft.

"Gee," Annie cried back to the sheriff, "they got away."

She had spoken too soon. Her voice had started a bedlam of voices from below.

Above all the rest rose "scaredy cat's" hysterical one, "Hey, let us out of here."

"Don't worry, we will." The sheriff who had paused to light a lantern bent over the hole to look at the pale upturned faces.

Ruff reacted to the situation far differently from "scaredy cat." His rage boiled over and most of it was vented on Sandy who grinned down at him wickedly.

"Just let me get my hands on that cur," threatened Ruff, but neither Annie or Sandy were frightened by him. His days of bullying were past.

"Hum," commented the sheriff. "Don't know any of them but Ruff. Any of you boys recognize them?"

There were conversations here and there but no one admitted having seen them before. The sheriff turned toward Halk, but he too shook his head.

"So, all strangers. Well, I suppose we've got to get them up. Can some of you boys rig up that windlass? We'll give them a ride up in that."

There were plenty of willing hands. It did not take long before the men were being hauled up one at a time, dropped at the edge of the shaft, and not very gently herded to the wall where two of the deputies took them in charge.

"So none of you know them?" The sheriff was try-ing to give Halk enough rope to hang himself.

The men were being loyal; they said not a word to him. In fact, they passed him with hardly a glance. But Halk was uncomfortable. He could feel the ac-cusing eyes of the men on him. As usual when he was in a tight spot he decided to talk his way out, and this time it was his undoing.

"Probably imported from New York," he told the sheriff. "Probably Burn hired them to do the job for him."

"That won't hold water. What about Ruff?"

"Well, you know the record he's got. Running off with his mother's money wasn't the last thing he pulled, I thought maybe I could reform him, but I was suspicious when he started leaving town every day."

That was enough for Ruff. "A fine one you are to talk," he spat. "At least I've never roped someone else into taking the rap for me."

That opened a flood of accusations, and they came too fast for even Halk to think up plausible answers. The men resented Halk's comfortable seat in town, covering up for them, while they did all the dirty work. He did get credit for all the planning, but the actual jobs were given to them.

"And he was taking the biggest cut, too," complained one of them.

"Well, I guess that's all the evidence we need," said the sheriff at last. "Those men will tell us anything more we want to know. Get them back to town."

The deputies divided the robbers among them so that there would be no chance of escape. Halk too was bundled off to one of the cars.

"I remember Uncle Jack saying that some people's polish wears thin awful fast," Annie told the sheriff as she watched Halk being ushered to the car. "He sure lost his in a hurry."

"Well, Annie, your uncle would know too, that you can't use a poor quality merchandise to begin with and expect a shiny coating to last on it. At that Gila's coat has worn well for too many years. He should have been caught a long time ago."

"It makes me sick the way people act like sheep, all following one person without using their own heads about it. They're what cause half the trouble in this world."

"I guess maybe that's right, Annie. If a man has a gift for gab he can make most anyone believe that black is white. Look at Hitler and Mussolini, they just did in a big way what Gila's been copying on a small scale."

"Anyway," Annie consoled herself, "they always do get caught finally. It's just too bad they can make so many suffer before they wind up their careers. If there were just some way to stop them before they got started."

"Don't worry, Annie, there will be. With so many people working on it, sooner or later we're bound to find a way to stop them."

They watched the cars bearing the criminals start down the mountain road, and then those who had remained headed back into the mine.

"The next thing is the money, I suppose." The sheriff had been far too busy getting the robbers to think about money.

"Part of it's easy."

Annie gave exact instructions. The sheriff called some of the men over, but it was Annie, not he, who did the ordering. Soon a group was headed over the narrow path to the miners' cabin, while another group stayed at the mine.

"I don't know anything about blasting," Annie told them, "but I think it's all ready. They were just waiting for Ruff to come so they could set it off."

"Come on, let's go take a look." One of the older men was excited. "I used to do the ticklish jobs up here when it was running. I can tell if it's ready."

It was like a game to some of them. The town which

had once been a mining town had had to turn to other jobs, and so had the men who had worked here. Now what had once been tiresome work seemed like a party to them.

The man who had done blasting before swung down on the rope as though it had been just a day instead of twenty years ago since he had done it. Others followed him down, and all of them would have gone if the sheriff hadn't stopped them.

"You act like a bunch of little boys on a holiday," he told them, and they grinned sheepishly. "Much as I hate to spoil your fun, there's work to be done. If they can set that thing off, they've got to have a faster way up than one by one on the windlass. We've got to get that ladder back."

With so many working the ladder got back into the shaft in a hurry, but the staples that held it were not so easy to handle. In her haste Annie had let them drop, and now they were nowhere to be found. Some of the men went down to the first level to hunt, and their torches moved back and forth over the passage-way a long time before all four of the staples were located.

The men from below had been back to report long before the ladder was ready. At last with everything set, they all trooped up from the mine but the one who had taken charge of operations. They brought the dynamite that had not been used and set it carefully outside the shaft house.

Soon the last man too came hastily up the lower ladder to be out of the way of flying rock. He stayed there though the rest yelled at him to get out of harm's way.

"This is all right," he called, but his voice was cut off by the gigantic explosion that echoed and re-echoed through the passageways.

He had been right. The noise was the only sign of the explosion that they felt. All of them were anxious to see the results. They crowded down to the first level, but the dynamiter refused to let them go farther.

"Give it a chance to clear out," he ordered.

That was hard work. It seemed forever before he started for the ladder and motioned them to follow. They were again like little boys on a picnic. They shoved and pushed to be the first ones down. Annie, in spite of being the heroine, was forgotten, and she was just off the ladder when the first ones reached the passageway that had been opened.

"Whew!" whistled one. "There it all is."

Annie turned the bend and saw the big chamber that had been shut off for twenty years. The men were clustered about a pile of boxes in one corner, while one of the fellows pried off its cover. It was the gold all right. Even from a distance Annie could tell that.

Annie Saw the Boxes of Gold

Triumphantly the men shouldered it and lugged it up the steep ladders. As they carried it out to the cars another similar procession appeared around the bend on the narrow mountain path. Both gold shipments had been accounted for.

The sheriff swung his car around so that it was in lead position, and with Annie and Sandy beside him headed the procession back down the mountain road.

"I still don't quite see how that all happened," Annie complained. "Was that cave-in accidental?"

"It must have been," the sheriff replied. His eyes were glued to the road. "Evidently Halk and whoever helped him hid the money in there planning to go back for it, and before they got back the cave-in happened. You know, there were several men injured in that. Not one of them's living around here if I remember correctly. That sounds as though maybe they had been the other robbers."

"And when they were well they cleared out, 'cause Gila had. That sounds as though it could be right."

"Then Halk must have needed more money; he probably ran through that he stole from the mine accounts long ago."

"So he came back to get what he had left."

"That's what it sounds like. Someone must have let the news slip that another gold shipment was being sent through and he had to have both. One wasn't enough for him."

"Well, all's well that ends well. I suppose it doesn't matter what he had planned to do so long as we got him."

"That's right, and we've got him where he can't talk himself out of it again."

The car crossed the railroad track and raced down the deserted street.

"Where is everyone?" wondered Annie, but she was soon to find out.

CHAPTER TWELVE

Their return to town was a triumphal procession. Annie in the lead car discovered long before they got there that the town *was* out in full force, grouped around the sheriff's office. Of course, they had known where the men were headed, and the first cars had come back with the prisoners.

It sounded from the muttering of the people as if they were in an ugly mood, the same kind of mood they had been in on the day of Uncle Jack's arrest. The deputies who had brought the men down from the mountain were now stationed around, some at the top of the steps, some at the edges of the crowd, their guns ready to use if necessary.

"I sure wouldn't want to be Halk today," Annie told the sheriff.

"No, I suppose not, but he's pretty safe at that. Those deputies of mine know how to keep the people in hand. Really, though, that's one man I wouldn't much mind the people getting hold of. I'm not in favor of individuals or groups taking the law into their own hands, but sometimes there are men that don't deserve as good treatment as our courts give them."

"The thing that makes me see red," said Annie,

"is that there's no way to make Halk pay for all the misery Uncle Jack's been through. Poor Uncle Jack living in fear of being discovered all these years! I'll bet that hurt him even more than the prison sentence."

The sheriff stopped the car in front of his office. When the crowd saw who it was, they left the jail and clustered around the car. Before Annie realized what was happening she had been helped out of the car and hoisted on to the shoulders of the town's tallest men, then paraded to the steps of the office.

"Gee," she cried. "Golly, let me down!"

But the men paid no attention to her and it was a very embarrassed little girl who was at last set on the office steps. From her vantage point above the heads of the crowd she discovered Uncle Jack with Miss Jens 'way at the edge of the gathering.

Annie tried to push her way through the crowd to them, but unlike the last time when the crowd had stepped aside to let her pass so that she wouldn't come near them, now they refused to make way for her. Each one wanted to pat her on the back, or in the case of some of the ladies, kiss her, which Annie disliked even more.

"Let me through," she ordered, but they paid little attention. She had to fight every inch of the way. At last she reached the safety of Uncle Jack's arms.

"Oh, I've been so worried about you, Uncle Jack.

I was afraid you'd think I'd gone off and left you."

"Goodness, Annie." Miss Jens was as excited as Uncle Jack. "We knew you wouldn't do that. We've been worried sick about you. We couldn't imagine what had happened."

"Yes, Annie," said Jack, hugging her to him. "I was afraid Halk had something to do with your disappearance. You're sure you're all right?"

"Of course, I'm all right. What about you?"

She stood back so that she could look at him. He didn't look ill treated.

"I had fine care. Once the sheriff decided I really wasn't guilty he did everything for me and Miss Jens here has been more than helpful."

"Why, Mr. Boot, I had to do something to make up for the way the town was treating you. I've been so ashamed of Butternut."

"Butternut's not such a bad town," Uncle Jack defended it. "They just didn't know how to deal with a smart crook, and in a way maybe that in itself shows something. They've never had to deal with one before."

The crowd had turned to the sheriff to get details of the capture. Very few of them were watching Annie and Uncle Jack. Miss Jens had appointed herself overseer of their affairs.

"Don't you suppose this would be a good time for you two to sneak out of here? The first thing you know they'll be pestering you with questions and you'll never get away from them."

"That's a good idea, Miss Jens. Come on, let's go home."

The three moved away from the crowd as quietly as they could. As soon as they were far enough not to be noticed they hastened their steps toward the little white house.

It was with a feeling of great content that they opened the door of the house. Uncle Jack headed for his leather chair and sank into it. "I didn't realize how attached I'd become to this," he told Annie. "Boy, it's good to get home."

"I'll say so!" echoed Annie. "I hope I never have to spend another night up on that mountain. Now to get something to eat, and then I'll be all comfortable."

"Don't you worry about that, Annie." Miss Jens had been planning this already. "I'll have something in a jiffy. I'll find something out there. You sit still."

"Oh, gee!" exclaimed Annie. "You know what I did, Uncle Jack? I took all the canned food up to the mine with me. I was afraid I'd have to hide out there for some time. And everything happened so fast I forgot about it. It's still up there, in those scrub pines."

"Don't worry about that. It'll keep. We'll go up to get it some day. I want to take a look inside that mine anyhow. The night I was up there they didn't leave the mine at all and I never got a chance to get inside. I haven't been in there for twenty years now."

"He sounds wistful," thought Annie. "I wonder if he wishes he were back in mining again."

Aloud she said, "You know, Halk talked to the sheriff about opening the mine again. O'course that might be just talk, an excuse for having men there. Do you suppose it could be opened again?"

Boot's eyes lighted. "I hadn't thought about that, Annie. There hasn't been anything taken out for twenty years, but there was still a lot in there. We had just opened that new section, the one that caved in, and it looked as though that was a humdinger."

"Let's do it, Uncle Jack. The men were all excited about just going into the mine again. They acted as though they'd be glad to be able to work it again."

"Not so fast; not so fast. Don't you know it takes money? We'd have to redo all that has been done so far. Those timbers aren't any too strong after twenty years, I imagine, and then we'd need all new equipment. That costs money."

"Well, if you want to do it, we'll find the money somewhere. People would be willing to lend it to you now, I'll bet."

"Don't worry about that now. There's plenty of time to think about it later. I've still got the shoe store, you know."

"You don't know about the shoe store, do you?"

Annie hated to tell him the mess it was in. Now that most of the troubles were clearing up, she hated to have to report one more thing.

"Oh, yes, I know about that. Miss Jens told me. It won't take long to clear that up. We'll be set for business again in a day or two."

"Are you sure you want to bother with it, Uncle Jack? Wouldn't it be easier if you wanted to do mining to let the store go? How did you happen on to shoe repairing anyway?"

"That's the trade I was taught in prison, Annie. The prisons don't let you go back out into the world unable to make a living honestly. It isn't a bad trade."

"No, but it's not your real work."

But for the time being the future had to take care of itself. Miss Jens called from the kitchen and hand in hand Jack and Annie went out to the first meal at home for a long time.

Miss Jens had done well. She had a good hot dinner and had even remembered Sandy. He was happily eating under the stove, his tail going lickety-split.

Annie couldn't help laughing in delight. It was just so good to be home and have everything, or almost everything, all right again.

Everything was even better the following day. Annie slept until close to noon. As she rubbed her eyes and looked at her clock she gave a start of surprise.

"Jiminy, I never slept this late before, except when I was sick. I wonder what Uncle Jack will think of me."

Putting on her robe she headed for the stairs. Without pausing she rushed into the living room to find a whole delegation waiting for her. She would have retreated in embarrassment, but Uncle Jack, grinning broadly, pulled her forward.

The sheriff, the bank president, and several other men whom she had never seen before were there. They all seemed to be in on some kind of secret that she didn't know.

"Annie," the sheriff beamed at her, "this is Mr. Sumner, president of the railroad."

The man whom the sheriff had pointed out cleared his throat.

"For the past twenty years, there has been a standing reward for any information leading to the locating of the money stolen in the train robbery here. Now with the new robbery, a like amount has been set aside as reward for the capture of the bandits and the return of the money. Since without any doubt you alone were responsible for their capture, and for finding the money stolen twenty years ago, the company has asked me to present you with this check."

He took out his billfold and slowly extracted from it a pink slip of paper. "This covers rewards for both robberies. We want to tell you how much in your debt we are."

Annie didn't know what to say. This had all come as a surprise to her. The only reward she had been looking for was Uncle Jack's freedom. She could handle the robbers, but this was a situation with which she couldn't quite cope. She could feel her face flushing, and the only words she could think of were "Thank you." Everyone else was so busy congratulating her that she didn't have to think of anything else to say.

"What's going to become of that money, Annie?" the bank president wanted to know.

"Well, I suppose first of all it had better be put in your bank," Annie told him.

The president blushed.

"I wasn't drumming up business. I really want to know what you're going to buy with it."

For the first time Annie glanced down at the check. It was made out for ten thousand dollars.

"Gosh! Leapin' lizards!" Annie's vocabulary wasn't big enough to show her astonishment. "I don't know." Her eyes were round with surprise. "That's a lot of money to know what to do with."

They laughed at her and Uncle Jack put a comforting arm around her. "Don't try to decide now," he warned. "There's plenty of time for that later."

"That's right." Annie was glad that there would be more time to consider.

The delegation left and Annie took the important pink check down to the bank. On the way she met dozens of people. Every single one wanted to stop to talk.

One of the first ones she met was Mrs. Speedle.

"We're all so happy about this Annie. I know how proud your Uncle Jack must be of you. There was something about that Halk that was just too good to be true. Even really important people couldn't be as perfect as he pretended to be. I decided at that party that he wasn't the author he pretended to be. He didn't know about any of the books we've been reading at our literary club."

"Miss Jens was right when she said that there wasn't a book by him then, wasn't she?" Annie had to take this chance to defend her friend.

"Yes, of course. That Mrs. Bart is so sure she's right. She got us all believing that Miss Jens didn't know what she was talking about."

"Sure, lay the blame on someone else," thought Annie, but she couldn't seem to dislike Mrs. Speedle in spite of all her gossiping.

"What are you going to do with all that money?" Mrs. Speedle was interested in knowing too. "That's a lot of money for a little girl to have."

"I haven't decided yet. I guess I'll have to do a lot of figuring before I decide what to use it for."

Annie had just about decided to what use she

Annie Deposited Her Check in the Bank

would put it, but that was going to be her secret for a while. Mrs. Speedle would be one of the last ones to know.

"Just because I'd like to see one time when she wasn't the first to know something," Annie thought.

After many interruptions she reached the bank and got her check safely deposited in a brand new account.

"I think I'd better find a spot to do some figuring," she decided, "and the best place for that is my stone up on the mountain road."

After having told herself that she wanted nothing more to do with that mountain here she was heading for it again.

"It is kind of fascinating," she thought. "You get so you can't leave it alone.

"I hope Uncle Jack won't worry. He just thought I was going to the bank, but I'll try not to be gone too long, and I've just got to figure all this out."

She refused to think about it until she was comfortably settled on her stone, looking out over the valley and Butternut.

"That money really belongs to Uncle Jack because he's the one who's had all the suffering. There's no way the state can make it up to him, even if Gila is caught. He's had all the punishment and nothing can take that away. At least he ought to get the reward. I know he won't let me give it to him though. There's

only one way and that's to put it in the mine. I'll bet
Mr. Bart could find a way for me if I asked him. I
know Uncle Jack would like to go back to mining
more than anything else. I've got to be sure he's going
to be happy, because some time I'll have to leave here,
and I'd hate to see him lonely and miserable again.
I want to be sure he's contented."

Full of her plans to help Uncle Jack before she had
to leave Butternut, she sat contentedly and watched
the lights start blinking on in the village below her.
Finally she heard the far-off lonesome whistle of the
evening train. It rounded the curve, the darkness
breaking away before it, and as it reached the mountain road it gave another little whistle that sounded
to Annie as though it were a specially friendly greet-
ing just for her.

"It *is* a pretty town, isn't it?" She wondered how
she could have been hating it so a day ago, and now
here she was loving it again. "It's one of the nicest
places I know, and I'll bet it will be even better when
the mine gets working again."

Happy at thinking about all the things that would
happen when her money opened the mine once more,
she walked down the mountain road back to the
town. She thought she saw someone in the path ahead
of her, and on looking closer she discovered it was
Mary Lou Bart.

"Hi, Annie," she called as Annie approached. "I

thought that was you so I waited. Can I walk home with you?"

"Why, sure, Mary Lou." Annie discovered that she didn't dislike her any more either and thought to herself, "Why, she must have a pretty unpleasant time of it. Her mother's so fussy about what she does. I guess she's not to blame for the way her mother brought her up. Maybe if *I'm* nice to her, some of the other kids will be friends with her too."

"Boy, I really like this town," she told the rather surprised Mary Lou. "I've only been here a couple weeks and I feel as if I belong here already."

But to herself she sorrowfully added, "It's too bad I can't just go on being a part of it. I suppose some day soon I'll find out where Daddy is, and then I'll have to go to whatever place he wants me to be. Maybe some day though I can come back and bring him with me."

So, busily planning ahead to a far-off time when she could return, she went back, for the short time she was sure was left, to the little white house that in a few days more than a week had come as close to being a home as any place she had ever been, and to the kindly white-haired man whom she had come to regard as her very own uncle.

WHITMAN
AUTHORIZED EDITIONS

NEW STORIES OF ADVENTURE AND MYSTERY

Up-to-the-minute novels for boys and girls about Favorite Characters, all popular and well-known, including—

INVISIBLE SCARLET O'NEIL

LITTLE ORPHAN ANNIE and the Gila Monster Gang

BRENDA STARR, Girl Reporter

DICK TRACY, Ace Detective

TILLIE THE TOILER and the Masquerading Duchess

BLONDIE and Dagwood's Adventure in Magic

BLONDIE and Dagwood's Snapshot Clue

BLONDIE and Dagwood's Secret Service

JOHN PAYNE and the Menace at Hawk's Nest

BETTY GRABLE and the House With the Iron Shutters

BOOTS (of "Boots and Her Buddies") and the Mystery of the Unlucky Vase

ANN SHERIDAN and the Sign of the Sphinx

JANE WITHERS and the Swamp Wizard

WHITMAN
AUTHORIZED EDITIONS

THE EXCITING NEW

FIGHTERS FOR FREEDOM SERIES

Thrilling novels of war and adventure for modern boys and girls

Kitty Carter of the CANTEEN CORPS

Nancy Dale, ARMY NURSE

March Anson and Scoot Bailey of the U.S. NAVY

Dick Donnelly of the PARATROOPS

Norma Kent of the WACS

Sally Scott of the WAVES

Barry Blake of the FLYING FORTRESS

Sparky Ames and Mary Mason of the FERRY COMMAND